From the Depths

An anthology

Edited by Mark Bilsborough

WYLDBLOOD

This edition published 2023 by Wyldblood Press, Thicket View, Maidenhead SL6 6PX

ISBN: 978-1-914417-15-3

Contents

Introduction

Barnacles and bilge rats – we're full of them. Mermaids, sea creatures, monsters from the deep, Pirates who ought to know better doing things that ought to be impossible. Selkies. Things with piercing eyes and tentacles – they're all here.

We're drawn to the sea. The last great unknown, at least on this Earth. More than 80% of the ocean is unexplored – and over 90% of sea creatures have yet to be classified (maybe more, in those uncharted murky, murky depths).

And these unknown monsters are going to seem like aliens to us. As if all those squid and octopus and great white sharks weren't alien enough. But deep down below, where the pressure would crush you in an instant and the dark is midnight black forever, life teems in abundance. Who's to say it's not intelligent? Who's to say it's not curious? Who's to say we won't see it one day wrapped around a ocean vessel or singing to us from sun kissed waves?

We're proud to present fifteen fine stories with a satisfyingly salty tinge and we hope you enjoy them.

After you've read them, you'll never look at the sea in the same way again.

Mark Bilsborough
Editor

Beneath the Glass Dark

N.V. Haskell

Knotting the rope around your ankles with bone-sore fingers, your gaze settles on the still water, and you hesitate. Is this truly the best way to avoid those good-intentioned neighbors who assault you with their unflinching opinions about *your* grief? They seem oblivious and undaunted by your awkward retreats.

And you're tired of their words. Exhausted in your soul.

The edges of the stone blocks scrape the planks as you drag them an inch closer to the edge of the pier. No, there is only one place you can think to go where they won't follow. The place where Isla would go when she needed to escape this world, back before she escaped it for good. Trust the magic she imparted to you, even if your faith in the universe is broken.

The ropes chafe your thin ankle flesh as you test them to ensure their strength.

Neighbors' voices creep from their open windows through the night air. When someone laughs with full belly relief, it cuts with a sharpness that emphasizes how separate you are. You do not remember the last time you laughed, nor the last time you wanted to enjoy anyone else's. Silence and grief have been your constant companions for long months in your empty home.

The parched skin of your knuckles cracks and bleeds as you struggle to pull the blocks the final three inches. Your limbs tremble, but you are sure that it is due to fatigue. Your breath is labored too, but that is because you have been stagnant for too many months and the effort is taking its toll. You spent too much of the long winter sitting beside the fire with your misery. Inactivity has made you weak.

These are the lies you tell yourself. You were always a good liar.

Especially to yourself.

You stumble backward, teetering on the edge for a moment before regaining your balance. Isla would chide you for that. She had always made this look easy, but this is your first time. You sit cross-legged on the rough boards and watch distant lanterns cast flickering light from neighboring windows.

Perhaps tomorrow the herbalist will stop appearing with their wares of oils, dried weeds, and nature-sharpened stones, in which they insist there is magic. But you felt no magic from any of their herbs or tinctures, and all the rocks ever did was cast sparkling prisms across the floor in the afternoon sunlight. How you resented them more for their well-meaning, but false, promises.

They never understood the quiet magic that filled your sister's being, that stuff that kept her strong longer than she ought to have been. And since they did not understand that, they have no right to know about her parting gift to you. Some magic is only passed through an innate understanding and deep longing for solitude.

"Where are you going?" you would ask her. Though you knew that when the sunlight grew short Isla would make her way to the lake and disappear for a few days or several weeks.

"To my other life," she would say softly with no intent to hurt, but it always did. You would act cold toward her when she left, then bundle yourself in coats and scarves and sit atop the pier, waiting for her to return. You regret your curtness toward her then, but she never resented you for it. It all seems so long ago now.

As much as you miss her, you surely will not miss the faith-driven neighbors who profess hallowed words and prayers full of inexperience and discomfort. They know nothing about life or death, hiding behind their unproven prayers with resolve that has never been tested. They cling to their faith like handfuls of straw, and you hope for a strong wind to twist it from their grasp and scatter it so that they might understand the frailty of existence.

There are others who express concern by intruding upon your doorstep with single bowl food creations full of pity. But you know they return to their homes and talk in hushed tones about your sorrow and anger, so you never answer the door. Instead, you let their food rot on the doorstep until they return and collect their putrid efforts. You hope their bowls are ruined, and they might not save them. You hope they grow to understand loss. To have it shake and rend them to their cores so that you can bring them a piteous casserole with too much salt and no flavor. You hope that…

No.

It's another lie you tell yourself as you swing your thin legs above the glassy dark water. You would not wish this hollow ache on any of them. Not really.

Still, they shouldn't try to force you from your sorrow. These people don't understand that when grief is all you have left of someone, you will fight to keep hold of it.

Your toes dip into the cool water, and a shiver wriggles up your legs. The rope strains against your calves and grows taut around the blocks that sit beside you while moonlight streaks through wispy clouds, spotting the skin of the water like soundless rain on a forest floor.

It's okay, you remind yourself, though you know that nothing will ever be the same. It's just another lie.

Your sigh lingers in the air as you stare down into the still depths beneath your feet. As you wonder about the catfish and the smallmouth bass that might be erratically swimming below, a chorus of toads begins their lover's calls.

Isla used to love those throaty cries. It was about this time of year that she would reemerge from the water and trudge into the house, dripping puddles behind her after a few weeks of submersion. She would wring out her dark algae-spattered hair entwined with hydrillas and wrap her lake-chilled arms around you. You would complain of the scent of fish and rotten eggs as you pushed her away. Then she would smile as if the weeks under water had reminded her of all that she loved.

When you were younger, you didn't understand why she needed to go away. It always felt personal, though Isla insisted it was not. But how could she claim to love you and also need to be away from you?

Now you know that it was never about you at all. Just like your actions have nothing to do with the neighbors now.

You shake your head then tip the stones over the edge. They crash through the water's surface as you follow them gracelessly, leaving ripples spiraling in your wake.

The frigid water steals your breath and shocks your limbs, locking your muscles tight. But air has been useless to you. You haven't really been able to breathe in months. Not since she died and left you hollow and gasping.

The stones sink for a long time, and you close your eyes as they drag away you from the streams of moonlight into the darkness. Isla insisted that there is nothing dangerous in this lake, but your heart flutters at all that cannot be seen. Eventually the stones settle upon the murky floor and the weight of the water squeezes the last of the air from you.

The final bubbles exit your mouth and dart upward, disappearing, but you are unafraid. You have Isla's breathless magic to keep you here as long as you like.

Finally, the environment reflects your grief. Silent and dark.

A day passes. You know this because golden rays illuminate the tendrils of the hydrillas and curly leaf pondweeds that sway in the water beside you. When the catfish nibble your toes, you kick them away but know that they will return to bother you, just like a cat. Shadows appear above. People stare down into the water, surely wondering where you have gone. But you are quiet and still, anchored, but floating in the drift.

Did Isla feel alone down here, or at peace? You don't notice when the water licks the tears from your eyes and carries them away.

By the third day, the catfish has claimed you as a point of interest and gathers friends to nip at your hair and your nails. They seem to enjoy the game of you pushing them away only for them to return but they disappear at night when something sleek and dark lingers nearby, assessing your resolve.

On the fourth day, most of the shadows above have returned to their lives, but one remains. That person lingers, sitting on the edge of the pier and occasionally blocking out the sun's rays as it travels across the sky behind them. They sit exactly where you spent long days waiting for your sister to reemerge from her self-imposed isolation.

That person sees you, that much is certain. They know you are hiding in the waters with your silence and your sorrow. But they do not bother you, and by the sixth day you find their presence comforting in its consistency.

On the eighth night, an eel brushes your hair and hisses in your ear, *'Give up your magic and join us.'*

But you do not reply. Your sister warned you not to trust the eels, and his words feel too desperate with want.

The next day, as you watch a snapping turtle swallow its slimy meal through the strips of light, the shadow above shifts. With a splash that sends the fish darting in calmer directions, a man swims toward you. The water has distorted and widened his face and colored him pale and wan. He resembles Isla. Why had you not thought of him these last few months?

He keeps a safe distance, but mumbles through the water with his little air. "Do you need anything?"

You shake your head, and his lips purse in concern.

With the last of his breath, he says, "I will be waiting when you are ready." He kicks his legs to return to the surface and climbs out. A minute later, his shadow resumes its post.

When you know that you are a broken thing, it seems strange to be valued. Loss has fragmented your ability to think, speak, or care for yourself or others. It is curious that he returns each day knowing that you are broken. And it occurs to you with some shame at the slowness of your realization, that he is probably shattered, too. Perhaps he does not need to be alone in the darkness like you do. It is even possible that he might have taken the advice of the faithful, or the concoctions of the herbalists, or the food of the gossiping neighbors, and you do not resent him for it. You would rather he had those tools than the incessant anger that had taken hold of your father during Isla's illness. Or the bottle that mother sank in to until it claimed her.

The eel now taunts you nightly, brushing your limbs with its slick body and leaving you no peace. It plays with your hair and eats its meals before your eyes so that bits of fish and frog float in front of your face while it gnashes its small sharp teeth.

'There is nothing left for you up there,' it whispers. *'You belong in the darkness. I have tasted the salt of your tears. If you wish to give them up completely, all you need to do is speak and you will never feel sorrow again. The creatures here do not linger*

on what is lost. Your sister knew this. She knew that you would belong with us.'

You shiver for the first time since you dropped to the lake's floor. But your lips remain tightly sealed. To speak to the eel is to resign yourself to staying in the darkness forever and there is comfort in the knowledge that someone waits for you above.

Days and nights slip past, and you lose track of how long you have been under these waters. You don't remember the last time you felt the breath of wind against your cheeks or saw the flutter of wings in a blue sky or felt the warmth of the sun upon your naked skin. These thoughts and the blooming desire for them overwhelm you.

The thought of leaving the quiet of the lake causes your heart to quicken. The neighbors would ask too many questions and you haven't been able to form complete sentences in months. So, you stay with the catfish and the curly leaf pondweeds and the hydrillas and watch the day turn to night from twenty feet below the water's surface. Up there, life goes on without you.

One night, the eel dons the illusion of your sister's features with grey eyes and dark hair hovering around her oval face.

'Stay with me,' it begs. *'I am lost and alone without you.'*

It is not her, no matter how much you want it to be. Isla would have understood why you hide, but she would not want you hidden forever.

'They do not know you as I know you,' the eel says as it encircles you. *'I need you.'*

Still, you say nothing. Words have so much power, yet so does silence.

When the shadow wafts across the water the next day, things change. Suddenly you want to tell him about the eel. You want to tell him why Isla hid down here so often before she became ill. Why it was in the throes of her sickness and struggle that she gave up her isolation and clung to the warmth of others.

Isla must have come to the same conclusion that you reach now. You both could handle the darkness and the whispers of the eel alone. That is easy. But when Isla was dying and knew that she would disappear, she needed the love of others to help her live. Her last months were filled with well-intentioned neighbors bringing their one pot dishes and garden flowers. The herbalists brought tinctures to ease her pain, while the faithful whispered prayers over her. She knew that there was nothing they could do, but perhaps it was that outpouring of care that sustained her longer than she ought to have lived.

You wave to the figure overhead. There are words to say, and he has been waiting all this time to hear your voice.

He dives into the water, like you used to do for Isla, and pulls out a knife from its sheath. The eel slithers around your feet while the catfish boldly swims back and forth before you, trying to lay claim to you. They hiss and chatter as he nears, but you shove them away.

The blade saws through the first rope, but he is already losing breath. He didn't get the same magic from Isla. You take the knife, and he darts upward as you sever the last rope.

'Don't leave me,' the eel cries.

The words wrench your gut, the same words that were whispered to Isla as she lay dying. You cannot speak to the eel and reassure it but, if you could, you would tell it that you'll return when the world overwhelms you again. And you know the eel will be waiting.

For now, you must live where the sun can warm your cheeks and the sound of the toads fill the night air. You must eat warm bread and wrap lake-chilled arms around those you love. You must remember to love.

You rise through sun-glittered water, with tendrils of hydrillas twisting in your hair, and break the surface. The blue sky and sharp light are blinding as strong hands wrest you up and on to the old pier where you flop gracelessly like a gasping fish.

A breath--your first in months--makes you cough.

"Sister?" He says.

The warm timbre of his voice is loud in ears that have grown accustomed to quiet. You wrap your arms around him, and he does not complain about your stench as he hugs you back. The sun kisses your cheeks while the wind brushes your skin.

You sit together and breathe while a toad calls from the shore.

N.V. Haskell is an award winning author published in Volume 38 of Writers of the Future, Deep Magic ezine, and the Of Wizards and Wolves David Farland Memorial Anthology. She lives somewhere between civilization and haunted caves with her long-suffering spouse, rescue pets, and too many squirrels that she can't help but feed. After many years working in healthcare, she continues to be stubbornly (or foolishly) optimistic.

Song of the Selmarin
Geraldine B Hunt

"You can give a siren your body," Gawen's father advised his only son. *"But do not give her your heart, for she will keep it forever."*

Far from land, astride a wooden deck heaving upon a restless ocean, Gawen braced himself against the ship's gunwale and tried to work out whether his new captain was a goddess or a monster.

She had raven-black hair wound into tight braids that swung like the tentacles of some exotic sea-creature. Her slim, sun-bronzed shoulders and delicate waist belied an unexpected strength. With eyes of crystalline ocean-blue, and a voice that worked on a man's mind like the fragrant incense of the islands from which she hailed, her name was Ahwenek.

She had captivated Gawen from the moment he met her on the docks at Stoke. Yearning for adventure and in serious need of coin, he had hoped to secure a position on her fishing boat.

"You look sturdy enough," Ahwenek said, scrutinising Gawen from toe to forelock. Her brilliant blue eyes ignited something inside him. "You know the prow from the beam? Your port from your starboard?"

Born from generations of rivermen, Gawen had grown up on the satin-brown waters of the Haven River; hauling salted fish from the seaport to the upper reaches, and returning with bundles of flax and sacks of winnowed grain. Despite this, the Selmarin fishing boat was like none he had encountered before. Constructed of strangely-patterned jungle timbers, with a defiant bowsprit, flared gunwales, and canted stern.

"I do," he croaked, so entranced by Ahwenek's voice that he almost lost his own. "Anything else, I'll learn."

"You will have to," she said. "We leave at first light tomorrow."

She's a goddess, he concluded in the unformed way of an eighteen-year-old who had just come into his strength and was not yet sure what to do with it. He packed his canvas duffel bag with no hesitation, and even less thought of his father's warning.

Now, further from land than Gawen had ever sailed before, he wondered whether he had made a perilous misjudgement. Ahwenek had drawn a curved blade from the tooled leather sheath tied about her waist, and was lustily slitting throats.

Her victims were dolphin-fish, and it was not the killing that disturbed Gawen, but the primal zest with which Ahwenek took their lives.

The fish were being hoisted aboard by the first mate: a mountainous man with corded arms and legs, and a bald head summing the muscular crest of his shoulders. Wedged in place on a teetering platform at the stern of the ship, he caught the fish with a flexible pole, twice his height, bearing a blunted hook and fluttering feathered lure.

Fish darted from the depths as if offering themselves for sacrifice. Each time a fish struck the lure, the first mate heaved upwards on the springy pole, catapulting the fish over his shoulder and into the boat. With a cat-like pivot, he then disengaged the hook and dropped the pole to the water again. Fish after fish, he delivered to Ahwenek, and she slaughtered them in a rhythmic ballet of blood and blade.

Gawen worked the deck pump, drawing buckets of seawater and sluicing the scuppers until they bled torrents of crimson foam.

Ahwenek's knife flashed back and forth, and all the while, she sang.

Her foreign tune danced fiercely across the blood-slick deck. It honed the morning sun to a more brilliant edge, and sharpened the salt-tang of the air. It confused Gawen's senses and made him lose track of what was right and what was wrong.

Jolted by a sudden thump on his shoulder, he turned to see the first mate grinning at him.

"Not heard the song of the Selmarin before, have you?"

Gawen shook his head.

"Best put your tongue away before some seagull takes a fancy to it, eh?"

Gawen snapped his mouth closed so quickly he almost bit his tongue off.

"Find the cook," interrupted Ahwenek, holding a fish by the tail. As its blood drained onto the deck, the flashing stripes along its flanks dulled to sluggish waves of grey and blue. "We shall honour this one."

Tilting an amused eyebrow at Gawen, the first mate strode aft to the galley.

They honoured the dolphin-fish by eating it in the Amnesian way: sliced thinly and tenderised in coconut milk, then seasoned with sea salt and island limes. Scooped from clam-shell bowls with curls of unleavened ship's bread.

As she ate, Ahwenek threw slices of fish to the ship's dragon, Regarde: an argent beast with aquamarine eyes, sharp, conical teeth, and a sinuous tail that lashed the deck. Acting as their scout, Regarde was sent regularly aloft to check for danger, or signs of schooling fish, or to guide the ship through shoals and reefs.

The rivermen of the Haven did not use dragons in the manner of the seafarers. To Gawen—who usually stepped well back when the royal dragons paraded past on ceremonial occasions—they were intimidating relics of Arcadia's past.

Regarde yowdled without warning and stood upright, unfolding her swooping, silver wings. With wings extended, the dragon was far larger than she appeared when tucked up in her night hatch, or curled about Ahwenek's shoulders.

She's magnificent, thought Gawen, even as he flinched.

His senses were humming with the taste of island spices, the confronting closeness of the dragon, and the captain's wild vitality. In comparison, life on the Haven River seemed so dull. Rivermen ate salt fish and wheat bread, with slices of dried pear. Sore backs and blistered hands were the worst dangers they faced. When the wind blew too hard, they sheltered in sandy coves behind convenient headlands.

His gaze returned to Ahwenek—so confounding in her beauty and her menace—and Gawen wondered whether he could ever again settle for the colourless existence of a riverman.

A sudden downdraft blew his forelock into his eyes. Regarde had taken flight. The dragon circled the mast and circled high above the boat. Her shadow passed across the deck as she soared towards the sun.

Pushing his hair aside, Gawen peered after her. Breath caught in his throat. To starboard, perhaps two miles off, a large dark shape broke the surface, became airborne for the span of two heartbeats, then fell back in a towering spray of foam.

"Sign!" yelled Ahwenek, springing up to the foredeck.

And now the horizon was churning with the silhouettes of large fish leaping from the ocean then crashing down again.

"Humpheads!" Ahwenek shouted. "Everyone on deck!"

The chaotic turbulence of water and flying fish was charging straight towards them.

The first mate leapt up to the helm and disconnected the lashings holding the ship's wheel in place. He ushered Gawen to the main sheet: a wrist-thick rope that restrained the mainsail. "Time to use those muscles for something other than rowing, Riverman."

The rest of the crew swarmed about the deck, tightening tie-lines and trimming the for'ard sails.

"Bear away!" Ahwenek cried.

As the first mate spun the wheel, the ship lurched and the main sail flapped once before crashing across to the other side. "Mainsheet on!"

Gawen gave the harsh rope a mighty tug that burned his palms. Another tug, and he locked the rope between the teeth of a wooden ratchet bolted to the deck. Wind filled the mainsail with an explosive snapping noise and drove the ship into the ocean swell.

"Hold course," said Ahwenek, lithely balanced on the bucking deck. Her voice was calm, but a sombre undertone chilled Gawen. "Boards up!"

Sailors heaved at winches to raise two leaf-shaped paddles hinged on either side of the boat. Gawen had seen them lowered into the water as rudders when sailing, but he now realised they also served as shields.

The school of humpheads was close enough for Gawen to make out their detail. Sturdy fish the size of large dogs, with jutting foreheads and indigo eyes. They rose in kaleidoscopic waves of colour, tails lashing as they leapt skyward, following some urgent compulsion known only to them.

The first fish hit the stern with a splintering thud. Another sailed straight through the rigging, barely avoiding an entanglement that could have brought the mast down. Saltwater sprayed across Gawen's face.

"Watch out!" yelled Ahwenek.

A heartbeat later, a slashing tail thwacked his shoulder and sent him reeling towards the rails. Churning waves reached for him as he flailed wildly for a hand-hold.

Ahwenek grabbed his arm and pulled him down to the scuppers. He fell prone, nose pressed against the deck. The planks reeked of fish and wood tar. Blood rushed from his thundering heart to his head. Fish scales rained upon him, and the ocean churned up through drain holes in the deck, and black shadows blocked the sun.

Gawen was gloriously aware of Ahwenek's presence: her quiet strength, and comforting solidity. The reverberating crashes and shuddering of the boat seemed to fade, as if some elemental force of nature had wrapped its arms around him.

Eventually the fish stopped coming.

When the collisions ceased, the first mate raised his head and scanned the ocean. "They're gone."

Ahwenek jumped up, leaving a sudden void by Gawen's side. He followed more slowly, still soporific from the effects of her proximity.

The reinforced ironwood stern of the boat had taken the brunt of the attack, and the paddle-shields had protected most of the rigging. One of the mast spreaders hung broken and twisted, and a sailor went swiftly aloft with a coil of flaxen rope to repair it.

The first mate brought the boat back on course, easing sheets and filling the mainsail as the paddle shields were lowered again.

Gawen noticed a lone humphead lying motionless on the foredeck. The length of a tall man's stride, with vibrant stripes and a battleram head. A humphead flying wrasse. Gawen had heard about them: massive schools of pelagic fish that roamed the ocean currents, following huge chains of jelly-like salps that spawned in the Selmarin sea. But the storytellers had done poor justice to the spectacle he just experienced.

A crewman raised his club to dispatch the wrasse.

"No," said Ahwenek. Dropping to one knee, she slipped her hands beneath the fish. Gawen expected her to draw a knife, but instead she carried the fish to the gunwale and climbed over. From a precarious hold on the narrow rubbing strake that ran along the hull, she dipped the fish into the sea. It hung dull and grey, great head sagging and fins wafting in the current.

"Too late," thought Gawen, realising she planned release it. But why would she waste so much fresh food?

"This fish is not meant for us," she said, as if reading Gawen's mind. She began to sing, in a tongue much different to her killing song.

These notes tingled through Gawen's body like lightning on a summer's eve.

Ahwenek's voice grew louder.

Colour crept back into the wrasse's scales. A sluggish wave of purple, then olive green.

The tempo of Ahwenek's song lifted.

Waves of colour rippled faster: through pink and yellow, then a sparkling emerald green. The fish's gills opened and closed. Its head moved.

Suddenly, the scales ignited with brilliant light. With a strong flick of its tail, the fish darted out of Ahwenek's hands and was gone.

Ahwenek climbed back aboard, and Regarde hopped across the deck, rubbing her head against the captain's side.

"Always take less than he offers," said Ahwenek, turning to Gawen. He knew she was speaking of Fjorte: the bringer of life, and explanation for all the mysteries of their world.

"It's the way." Ahwenek rubbed Regarde between her stubby horns. The dragon closed her eyes and chirred. "The balance."

Until now, Gawen had spared little though for the balance of the world. Farmers ploughed land for their crops, and slaughtered stock. Musselmen chiselled shellfish from the rocks. Flaxmen scythed wild-growing plants. Arcadia had always been a land of abundant riches and marvels, all for the taking. But if he were to believe Ahwenek, there were rules to be obeyed. Harvesting that had come so naturally now seemed irresponsible.

Gawen wondered why nobody had told him about this balance before.

"Unusual to see the humphead wrasse schools this far north," said the first mate, "but this is an unusual season."

"How so?" asked Gawen.

"Sea currents are all wrong. Should be a cold northerly current, but the ocean is warm. Water's rushing up from the Selmarin and washing the salps with it. Brought us up here to your parts, too.

"We tried to maintain course for the islands, but the wind was fickle, swinging the moment we had our sails set. Eventually, we gave in and let the current take us where it would. The stars showed we were making a great deal of north, but we did not realise how much east. Regarde went up every morning to look for signs of land, and one day she came down with a loud skarking cry, and there was the ironpot reef at the mouth of the Haven River."

Gawen recalled the day the ship sailed into his home harbour, and Stoke's townsfolk had turned out to witness the unexpected sight.

"Only one thing will push a ship against the wind," said the first mate, "and that is the Selmarin's hand planted firmly on her arse." He drew a carved ivory pick from a leather braid about his upper arm and probed the recesses between his teeth. "Selmarin's an odd and ancient sea. She mostly bides her time, all sluggish and sleepy, but once in a seafarer's lifetime her deep water boils up. Along with everything that lives in it."

"Like the salps," mused Gawen.

"And the humphead wrasse, yes." A complex expression narrowed the first mate's eyes. "And those that follow the wrasse."

"What do you mean?" asked Gawen, unsure whether the first mate was serious or joking.

The first mate gestured at the ocean surface, which had grown unnaturally calm after the earlier maelstrom. "Didn't you wonder what makes a big fish leap out of the water so furiously?"

"I assumed they were attacking us. Or hunting."

"They didn't attack us, Riverman, we just happened in their path. And they weren't hunting. They were being hunted."

Suspicious he was being taken for a fool, Gawen held his tongue.

"For all we know, what was hunting them is also hunting us," said the first mate, staring pointedly over the side of the ship.

Gawen refused to indulge the man by following his gaze, no matter how badly his instincts urged him to find out was down there. No matter that, all of a sudden, he wanted to know this *very much*.

"No point worrying. There's nothing we can do to stop it." The first mate slapped Gawen good-naturedly on the shoulder, then returned to the helm.

That night, Gawen lay sleepless in his bunk while dark waters whispered along the hull just inches from his head, like the ghosts of drowned sailors.

What was he thinking, to trade the reassuring shallows of the Haven River for this unfathomed ocean? For the creature they called their captain, and whatever other creatures might be hunting them from beneath? He thought of his parents, in the tiny cottage where he was born, lulled to sleep by the rippling Haven River. Would he ever hear that rippling lullaby again?

Next morning, the westing wind abated.

"She'd better blow again soon," said the first mate, "or we'll need your rowing skills to get back home, Riverman."

"Home?" Something clenched inside Gawen: longing or regret, he wasn't sure. "So soon?"

"Those barrels of salted dolphin-fish aren't going to sell themselves. We need to turn them into coin, and Stoke's our closest market."

While they waited for the wind to return, the crew stowed away fishing gear, spliced worn ropes, and checked the ship's timbers for rot. The ocean turned oily grey beneath spreading cloud cover. After several hours, dark ruffles appeared on the mirror-like surface.

"Wind's coming," said the first mate.

Gawen was packing tarred hemp between two warped planks of Regarde's night hatch when a strong breeze blew across the deck.

"Easting!" said Ahwenek. "Set course for the coast."

The first mate spun the wheel through a full turn, jibing the boat around. With billowing sails, she glided gently before the wind, her bow rising and falling to a soft rush of parting water.

Regarde perched beside Ahwenek on the bowsprit, while Ahwenek's voice flowed aft like a tidal surge. The lofty, thrumming cadence of it boosted Gawen's spirits.

It was an epic song, he imagined, of great deeds and hearts. Of lovers, and longing, and salvation.

"Is she singing to Fjorte?" he asked the first mate. "To keep us safe on the way home?"

The other man coughed a short, humourless laugh. "She is singing to keep us safe. But not to Fjorte."

"Who, then?"

"To him." The first mate gestured over the side of the ship.

In the depths, Gawen saw something new. A rush of blue on blue, shadows filling a void where before there had just been dark water. He had rarely known fear, but now it slithered through his gut and stole the strength from his limbs.

They were not alone.

Ahwenek raised her hand and released a shower of glittering fish scales, which danced and sparkled in the ship's frothy wake. The tone of her song changed. Now, it sounded less like victory and more like surrender.

No, thought Gawen. Not surrender. Oneness. This was a song of balance, and belonging. Like predator and prey?

In the shadowy void beneath the boat, Gawen searched for the creature that hunted them and finally found it. A huge, black eye, and sinuous tentacles trailing behind a vast body that moved as fluidly as the water itself.

A kraken.

Sunlight tripped through the swell created by its massive bulk. It was longer than the ship.

The kraken rose towards the surface, disturbing the trail of fish scales Ahwenek was casting from the bow.

Gawen's heart beat painfully against his ribs. He dared not breathe.

Ruffling the surface without breaking it, the sea-beast kept pace beside the boat.

The other crewmen watched as silently as Gawen.

Only Ahwenek seemed oblivious. Eyes closed, she swayed gently against the argent dragon.

The kraken rolled and lifted a barnacle-encrusted tentacle. An ammonia-stench rose with it. Water cascaded from gaping tooth-rimmed suckers. The tentacle slapped the surface and sent a wave crashing into the ship's hull.

Shuddering, Gawen clenched his teeth. He desperately wished to meet the next few moments with dignity, but was not sure he could. Would his mother and father ever learn how he had died? He braced for the attack.

But the kraken swam past without a glance. The massive tentacle retreated, leaving an oily slick as dark waters closed above it. With a single turn of its enormous body, the sea-beast melted back into the depths.

Gawen drew an agonising breath. Had it really gone?

Raising her head, Ahwenek cast a lilting tune up from the waves to soar through the rigging and take flight on the freshening wind. The tip of Regarde's serpentine tail curled back and forth in rhythm with the song.

At that moment, Gawen realised Ahwenek was no more monstrous or god-like than nature itself.

And he was no longer a riverman.

He was ready to give her his heart, his body, and anything else she required if he could sail with her forever. In balance with the world. Warded by the song of the Selmarin.

Wherever the ocean currents bore them.

Acknowledgement: This story would not have been possible without the inspiration of my sister, Kate Le Bars.

She first imagined the world of Arcadia, in which we have spent hundreds of happy hours as co-authors of other tales.

Geraldine B Hunt is a retired veterinarian and lover of fantastical animals: real and imagined. She has sailed and swum over much of the South Pacific, and is still hoping to catch a glimpse of Dr Dolittle's great glass seasnail. Her short stories have appeared in Aurealis, Sistership, and Litopia's Short Story Hunters. Pitfalls in Small Animal Surgery, an 80,000 word personal narrative of her career as a vet in Australia and the United States, was published by Wiley in 2017.

The Sea's Bones
D.K. Latta

The windows of the dining cabin teemed with rivulets like racing ants, the massive balloon overhead doing little to dissuade the pelting rain. Lightning fissured the roiling black clouds, briefly reflecting off the ocean seething beneath the airship. A thunderous clap rolled in hard on the heels of the lightning, shuddering the windows

The seated man stared impassively out at nature's ire. At least his body conveyed imperturbability; broad-shouldered but arms relaxed, dressed in a black long coat. His features were impossible to read, however. His head was swathed in bandages, save his mouth and chin, his eyes hidden behind Inuit-style snow goggles.

"Do you mind?"

He looked up at the young woman standing tentatively, hands gripping the back of one of the empty chairs at his table. Stirred from his brooding, he was once more aware of the tinkle of wine glasses, the tuxedoed musician sawing mournfully on his violin in the corner. There were tables devoid of diners (the rocking of the great air vessel clearly having depressed the appetite of some of their fellow passengers). Nonetheless he nodded. Grinning, she laid her stole across the chair's back and sat. She was unarguably attractive, with dark, inquisitive eyes, her black hair cut in a stylish bob. "I hate eating alone -- I'd just end up fretting about the weather. I'm Park Sung-mi, *Seoul World News*."

He stiffened, suspecting she was after more than simply a dining companion. Nonetheless, he decided to prolong the pretence. "I'm-"

"Declan Lefebvre," she said bluntly, still smiling. "I asked the purser when we embarked at Hong Kong, just to be sure. I'd have recognized you under normal circumstances and of course in your current..." She hesitated, fumbling for words as she gestured vaguely in his direction.

"Guise?" he suggested drily.

"I read about your accident in -- the Andes, wasn't it?"

"I'm afraid I'm not currently doing interviews," he said politely.

"I'm just naturally inquisitive," she said, unoffended. Smiling slyly, she added: "Though perhaps I'll change your mind before we arrive in San Francisco."

Declan simply dipped his head noncommittally.

"Thank God for some life!" Without waiting to be invited a third figure settled at their table. Though the bushy mutton chops advancing fiercely across his face were snow white, he appeared robust, pipe clenched between teeth. He smelled, incongruously, of machine oil. His eyes swept critically about the subdued diners scattered about the cabin. "It's like eating with a bunch of bloody mummies." He flinched as he glanced at Declan. "Ah...no offense, old boy."

"The storm is making everyone pensive, Sir Marshall," said the woman. "I'm not sure why we can't just rise above it."

"Damned fool captain probably took on too much cargo or passengers," he said authoritatively, unsurprised she knew his name. "Retards the buoyancy. As for this little sprinkle, I was in Indian during the monsoon of 1893 -- or was it 1895? Now *that*, young lady, was a storm." He shifted his pipe from one corner of his mouth to the other. "Still, if we're going to eat together we might as well know each other. Sir Marshall Wynn-Burr, London -- though really a citizen of the world, you could say."

"Ex-soldier, Peer of the Realm, big game hunter," the woman rattled off as though reading from a teletype. She repeated her own name and credentials, then gestured at the bandaged man. "And this is Declan Lefebvre, of Canada -- though like us, more of a world traveller. You've heard of him? He's something of a professional adventurer."

"Can't say as I have," sniffed Sir Marshall. "Adventurer, eh? Ever bagged black rhinos in South Africa-?"

"Not *that* kind of adventure, Sir Marshall," she politely interrupted. "You perhaps heard of the Howard Arkham expedition that was lost in the Andes a few weeks ago? It was Mr. Lefebvre here who went in and brought them out."

Sir Marshall grimaced at the allusion to the other man's heroism. "Yes, I *suppose* I heard of that. Mind you I was on a hunting trip in the jungles of Borneo at the time, else I might have got involved myself. That what happened to your face?"

"Sir Marshall!" objected the woman.

"It's all right," Declan said. "And -- yes. I was caught out in an ice storm for a day and a half, with lashing winds. Had much of my skin basically sandpapered off. A local witch doctor provided me with a poultice that he suggested I keep applied to my face for a month or two, which might repair the skin." He shrugged. "I guess time will tell."

Sir Marshall harrumphed. "Don't cotton with savages and their ointments and superstitions. Give me good old European industry any day." He plunked his left elbow on the table and rolled back his sleeve, revealing the steel rods, bolts, and pistons of a mechanical arm -- explaining the odour of lubricating oil clinging to him like cologne. "Got my arm mauled by a lion on the Serengeti. Local witch doctor tried to sell me on cleaning out the gashes and sewing it all back together. Poppycock! When I got back to old Blighty I had the whole arm chopped off and 'Bessie' here slapped on in its place. Good as new -- better even." Just then the limb farted a puff of steam through a release valve on the metal biceps. "Uh, excuse me," he said politely, rolling his sleeve back down.

"Is everything all right?" a sepulchral voice rolled over them.

For all his size the figure had moved as soundlessly as a ghost. He loomed a good eight feet tall, his tuxedo straining to constrain his broad chest, buttons attached with twine. His face and large hands were exceptionally hirsute and his flat-nosed, toothsome features were decidedly bestial.

"Yes, thank you, purser," said Sung-mi, speaking for all of them. The lights flickered. "We are quite safe, aren't we?"

"Certainly, madam," he growled courteously. "The East India Airship Line has one of the finest safety records in the world," he explained, as though having recited it more than once to fretful passengers this evening.

"Why *are* we flying so low?" inquired Declan.

"Sir Marshall here suggested we were too heavy," Sung-mi said, locking eyes with the giant purser.

"I'm sure the flight crew know what they're doing," he said reassuringly, but vaguely. "The *Romeo* is the most advanced vessel in the sky."

"And the *Juliet*?" Sung-mi said with deliberate nonchalance.

The purser hesitated.

"There's a sister ship, isn't there? But I don't believe she was put into rotation after her shakedown cruise."

"You must be quite the airship buff, madam," he said, though having access to the passenger manifest he was doubtless aware of her profession. "As I understand it, the *Juliet* is undergoing minor refits."

Before she could press further, Sir Marshall grumbled, "The service here is abysmal, boy. No one's been around to take our orders."

"I do apologize, sir. Unfortunately with the storm many of the passengers chose to sup in their cabins, so we are spread unavoidably thin."

"I remember when the service staff on airships was primarily trained monkeys," Sung-mi said.

"Bonobo apes," the purser corrected. "And, yes, they were hardy little workers. However it was decided high altitudes were not conducive to their constitutions and the switch was made to human staff."

"'Decided!'" snorted Sir Marshall. "Bullied, you mean. Animal rights activists started marching and picketing, just like those damned suffragettes before them, and the Board of Directors of the EIAL caved like a bunch of pansies. That's why ticket prices have gone up, don't you know. Can't pay humans in bananas, not without yet another hue and cry -- more's the pity."

"Ah...yes," the purser observed neutrally. "I'll see about hurrying your server." The towering figure turned, hesitated, then looked sheepishly at Declan. "I hope it won't seem impertinent, sir, but it is a great pleasure to have you on board. I'm well aware of all that you've done and tried to do for my people over the years."

Despite his features being obscured, Declan seemed momentarily embarrassed. Then he held out his hand. "Well...thank you, uh...?"

"Pericles," said the purser, folding his big hand around Declan's almost as though it were a child's in comparison.

After the purser departed, Sung-mi turned to Sir Marshall. "Mr. Lefebvre here was supposed to have been instrumental in having the Sasquatches recognized as legal citizens by the Canadian parliament." She looked at Declan. "One story I heard was that you dangled the prime minister by his ankles from a window until he agreed. But I suppose that's probably apocryphal."

"Probably," Declan said.

Sir Marshall harrumphed. "I'm sure you know best," he told Declan. "But I wonder where it will end. Giving dogs the vote? Forcing people to marry their daughters to cats?"

Sung-mi opened her mouth, then pursed her lips, and joined Declan in mutely looking out the window.

Declan stirred under starched sheets. No moonlight filtered through the porthole as rain lashed the hull, albeit less fiercely than earlier. Another tentative knock reminded him what had roused him. He donned his house coat, checked that his bandages were still secure, then retrieved his snow goggles. His light sensitivity was another result of the Andes expedition -- ironic, he mused bitterly, that a man accustomed to the wilds of northern Canada should suffer his worse cold-related injuries in a southern region.

He cracked open his door.

"I'm terribly sorry to wake you, sir," said the giant purser in a hushed voice. "It is most presumptuous of me, but we've developed a bit of a," he hesitated, "difficulty."

"Quite all right, Pericles," he said, also affecting a subdued tone, the purser presumably not wanting to rouse others. This was not the first time Declan's reputation had resulted in his advice being solicited over some local contretemps. "What's the matter? And, please, call me Declan."

"Of course, sir -- thank you. Well, Mister Declan sir, Miss Park's earlier comment about the altitude sort of nagged at me; then I noticed that according to my compass we were off course. I was not unduly concerned, assuming the captain was endeavouring to circumnavigate the storm."

"Did he confirm this?"

"That's rather the crux of my difficulty, sir. I cannot get a response from any of the bridge crew -- and the door to the bridge is locked."

Declan stiffened. "Are we drifting?"

"I think not, sir."

So the ship was under control, but the bridge unresponsive. Declan cinched the belt of his house coat. "Why don't you take me to the bridge, Pericles?"

A door whispered open a few cabins down and Sung-mi poked her head out. "What's going on?"

The purser straightened his massive shoulders, "Oh, nothing, madam. We were just-"

"Pericles," interrupted Declan wryly, "best to tell her now. She'll just try to find out on her own anyway."

Pericles guided Declan and, if only unavoidably, Sung-mi through the grey shadows of the corridors, the gas-lamps at their lowest ebb to enhance the nocturnal atmosphere. Most were asleep, so there was something surreal about wandering this pinnacle of human ingenuity seeming forsaken by humanity. The purser led them through one doorway, leaving the passenger areas behind, and then another, before finally bringing them before a sturdy mahogany door affixed with the sign "No Unauthorized Personnel Beyond This Aperture."

Declan nodded at the giant purser who unhooked the speaking hose from beside the door and blew into it. Faintly they heard the resulting whistle on the other side of the door. But no one responded.

An omnipresent murmur underscored everything, composed of the ship's engines, the storm, the creaking and groaning of the vessel's structure as it was battered by the winds. It was impossible to state with any confidence if there were sounds of the bridge crew moving beyond the door.

Declan rapped upon the door. "Captain?" Then louder: "It is imperative that we have a moment of your time, please!"

"Perhaps a less impersonal approach?" suggested Sung-mi. "What's the captain's name?"

"I'm afraid I don't know," said Pericles. "The captain -- and indeed the bridge crew -- embarked whilst I was occupied with other duties."

"You never met any of the bridge crew?" demanded Sung-mi. "Is that normal?"

"No, madam. However as purser technically my function is primarily to concern myself with the passengers."

Declan tried the door handle.

"What are you thinking?" prodded Sung-mi after a moment. "A gas leak? Or do you suspect a hijacking? Anarchists? Cultists?"

Delcan nudged aside a porthole curtain. It was greying outside, suggesting the storm was abating and dawn was aborning -- but with no clue where over the Pacific they might be. "I'm thinking we need to get that door open." He threw his shoulder against the door.

"Confound it, what are you up to, man?!" Sir Marshall exclaimed, coming up behind them. His white hair sprang out from his head in odd directions, an expensive house coat of scarlet and black wrapped about him. "I've been wandering this blasted balloon trying to find someone to wrestle me up a cup of tea only to find you three blighters trying to shanghai the bloody thing."

Sung-mi quickly explained the situation to the newcomer. He harrumphed sceptically. "Nonsense. The boy here told us the EIAL has a perfect safety record." He shouldered past the others and pounded on the door with his flesh hand. "Ahoy! Sir Marshall Wynn-Burr here! Get the wax out of your ears and come speak with us, if you can be bothered!"

Silence answered him.

"Hmmm. I suggest we shake the wireless operator out of bed and get a message to the company. I'm sure it's just a new protocol or some such thing."

"We can't be sure we are in range of any receivers," explained Pericles. "And the longer this goes on, the farther afield we'll stray."

Declan once more threw his shoulder against the door. He looked toward Sir Marshall. "Perhaps you might assist?" He did not ask Pericles. As an employee he was in a precarious position when it came to damaging company property. And Sasquatches were, by temperament, pacifists.

Sir Marshall chewed his cheek a moment, then: "Confound it -- all right. But this is on you three. I'm not paying for damages." He stepped forward and, with a hiss of pistons, drove his metal fist through the door. Then he gripped the handle on the other side and wrenched. Declan carefully pushed the door, ready for anything.

The dim room beyond offered only the hushed susurration of machinery.

Tentatively Declan stepped over the threshold. "No one's here."

Pericles adjusted the flow of one of the gas lamps, illuminating the room as the others spread out. The front and sides were comprised mostly of plate glass from the waist up, providing a view both spectacular and unsettling, since it reinforced that there was nothing to be seen in the grey dawn save the restless waves. There was a dais in the centre of the bridge, and panels before the windows that would be the posts for the various crew. At the front was a massive wheel that continued to roll one way and then the other, casually guiding the vessel as though by an invisible helmsman.

Large vacuum tubes sprouted seeming at random from panels, almost like fungal mushrooms growing wild in a damp basement. Cables draped from the ceiling like jungle vines. Two rigid wires jutted upright from one panel and tendrils of electricity danced between them. It was as if someone had crudely modified a conventional airship bridge with instrumentation for some, as yet, undecipherable purpose.

"Oh my God!" Sung-mi covered her mouth as she stood before the centre dais. As he stepped forward Declan realized the surface of the dais was glass and it was, in fact, a tank filled with liquid.

Something rested within the liquid.

"What is *that*?" asked Pericles, looming over his shoulder.

"It's...a brain," Declan said flatly, articulating what they could plainly perceive. Nor was it any brain, if such a thing could be thought absent irony considering the circumstances. It was enormous.

"Who -- *what* is it?" stammered Sung-mi. "Why is it here and not in the hold, on its way to a museum, or to some freakshow? And for heaven's sake: where's the bridge crew?"

Declan scanned the bridge, the helm wheel continuing to adjust itself as though steered by invisible hands, the cables running along the floor from the tank. "I think a crew was never here," he said. "And this *isn't* cargo."

Sung-mi gaped at him, then at the brain. "This is running the vessel?"

"In the dining cabin, you said something about the *Romeo* being a new design?"

"Uh, yes, sir," said the purser, momentarily relieved at the conversation turning to something within his purview. "The *Romeo* and the *Juliet* are state-of-the-art, luxury airships. The face of the-" he hesitated, "uh, of the future."

"And what exactly happened to the *Juliet*?"

"She went out on a shake-down voyage," said Sung-mi, "but has yet to be put into regular service."

"She needed some minor re-fitting," Pericles added. He shrugged his huge shoulders. "At least that was the scuttlebutt."

"So something happened on her maiden voyage requiring her to be pre-emptively pulled from service -- and she's the same design as the vessel we are currently on?"

Pericles said nothing. Sung-mi stared wide-eyed. Sir Marshall simply harrumphed.

For a time the four stayed on the bridge, uncertain what to do. They had, however, decided what *not* to do. They concluded it was best not to inform the passengers or the rest of the crew -- the latter whom would already be about, preparing for the former who would shortly be stirring. Until they had more information, they would merely incite a panic.

As for what to do? That was less clear. Pericles had already returned from the radio room, but without having raised anyone on the wireless; whether that was a result of the storm still thundering away on the horizon, their own geographical isolation, or perhaps some damage incurred during the night, they could not be sure. They could attempt to disengage the monstrous brain from the vessel's controls -- but that might manufacture an even greater crisis, leaving them entirely at the mercy of the elements. The brain had, at least, kept them on an even keel throughout the night.

"What is it, do you think?" Sung-mi asked weakly.

Declan turned from where he had been staring out the forward window. "What?"

"The brain. It's so big."

"They can do all sorts of things with science these days," Sir Marshall offered, snagging his thumbs under his house coat's lapels. "Creating an artificial brain is just a matter of dropping some cells on a petri dish and adding some fertilizer. I mean, it's a tad more complex, I suspect. But that sort of principle."

"Can we be sure it is artificial?" suggested Pericles

Sir Marshall grimaced. "It's a giant brain plugged into an airship. *Of course* it's artificial, boy -- use whatever brains you have in that furry noggin of yours-"

"Sir Marshall," Declan said dangerously, no longer biting his tongue, "if you refer to Mr. Pericles as 'boy' one more time I'll-"

"Out the window, sir -- look!" exclaimed the purser.

Declan swung about, half suspecting Pericles was simply deflecting the conversation before things became any tenser.

However, just breeching the grey-washed horizon was a small, dark shape thrust up from the ocean. An island, in the middle of nowhere. That suggested an explanation for the vessel's low altitude – had it been looking for something? "Perhaps there's a method to its madness." He looked at the brain. "I was too focused on what was happening, not on why. But I think your question is entirely germane to the situation. What is the origin of this brain?"

"Told you: cooked up in some mad scientist's lab, I don't doubt," huffed Sir Marshall.

Declan ignored him and looked from Sung-mi to Pericles. "It's no human brain, that's true enough. But think about what we're in -- an airship, often colourfully referred to as the 'leviathans of the skyways.'" He waited.

Sung-mi's eyes widened. "You mean -- a whale's brain?"

"It makes sense." He checked himself. "I mean, as much as anything makes sense in this nightmare. It's already accustomed to controlling a massive body, operating in a three-dimensional space rather than the two-dimensions a land animal thinks in; the winds are like currents, and so on."

"But how could you get it to operate properly?" asked Sung-mi. "Arrive where it was scheduled, that sort of thing?"

"How do you train any beast?" said Pericles. "Carrot and stick."

"What carrot could you offer a...?" She gestured helplessly at the tank.

"Mostly stick, then," Pericles said darkly.

"But -- but that's awful," Sung-mi said, looking for the first time at the disembodied brain not with horror, but pity.

"How does that explain that island?" Sir Marshall demanded sceptically.

Declan looked forward again. "I fear we'll only understand that as we get closer."

Suddenly a horrific scream blasted the air. The four doubled over, clapping hands over ears; the din so overwhelming it was almost a physical presence, pulsing through the deck boards, vibrating in their gums.

"What-?" shouted Declan, trying to be heard above the cacophony.

"It's the sound system, I think!" roared Pericles. "The emergency collision alarm -- but distorted! I've never heard it like this -- or so loud!"

"Turn it off!" wailed Sung-mi, crumpling to the floor.

Feeling like his head would explode, Declan stumbled about the room, trying to locate the mechanism that controlled the alarm. Seeing what he was attempting, Pericles staggered toward one panel. With his more-than-human strength he wrenched off the plating and swept one massive arm through the exposed wires and vacuum tubes.

,l;Abruptly the sound ceased. For a moment the sudden implosion of silence was almost as painful as the noise itself.

Sir Marshall leaned against a window, gasping. He peered outside, then slowly wheeled about, taking in the airship's immediate vicinity. "There's nothing to be seen anywhere."

Declan helped Sung-mi to her feet. "Pericles, you'd better go speak to the crew and passengers -- no point in keeping them in the dark any longer; not after they heard that. And ready life boats -- just in case."

As the purser left, Sir Marshall knuckled his ears. "If there's nothing we're about to collide with, then what the blazes was that all about?"

"Whale song?" Sung-mi suggested tentatively. "But why? And who was it calling to?"

All three turned to regard the dark shape on the horizon.

The island thrust from the ocean like Poseidon's crown, as if some giant king-of-the-seas lurked unseen below the water's veneer, the ocean dark and impenetrable under the overcast sky. Waves frothed against the ebony shores of basalt, before the island heaved upward into craggy, black cliffs. There was little vegetation to be seen, just glistening patches of moss and unhealthy looking seaweed where the stone met the water.

It was impossible to tell if anything grew amid the shadowy crags of the island's interior.

The area of the land mass was not great -- Declan suspected a man could pace out the circumference of the island in an hour or two. Yet by implication it was awe-inspiring. An island is the peak of a mountain or long dormant volcano. Given they were in the middle of the ocean, with no other land to be seen in any direction, this isolated tor must sit atop the brow of a gargantuan mountain indeed -- one that dwarfed the Himalayas or the Canadian Rockies as Jupiter dwarfed its moons. It was a vestibule to the deepest plateaus of the ocean, a realm man could, with all his technology, only imagine.

"Why drag us here?" asked Sung-mi so quiet it seemed almost subliminal. She stood next to Declan, as if drawing some comfort from his proximity, while Sir Marshall and Pericles stood around them, all four gaping out the window.

Pericles had done his best to reassure the passengers and his fellow crew members alike. He had seen that tea (liberally enhanced with brandy) was distributed while others of the crew readied the lifeboats in case the situation became irreversible.

Declan stirred and looked at Sung-mi, then his gaze slid past her to their white-haired companion. "Perhaps Sir Marshall has a theory."

Sir Marshall started. "Why would you think-?"

"You know more about what's going on than you let on," Declan said. "It only sunk in gradually. But you've been quick to try and stymie conversations that delve too much into the workings of these new ships. When Sung-mi tried to press Pericles about the fate of the *Juliet* at dinner, you started grousing about the service; when they speculated about the brain, you immediately insisted it was just the product of a lab experiment. Even your claim you were out looking for a cup of tea when you encountered us outside the bridge was implausible. I'm guessing you heard us in the corridor and followed -- whereupon you urged us to radio the company rather than investigate ourselves."

All three stared at the older man. His face was as impassive, as unreadable as Declan's bandaged one. Then he snorted. "Well what of it? I've done nothing wrong. You think I'd be on this bally thing if I knew it was going to go AWOL like this?"

That, at least, smacked of honesty.

"So what's your connection?" asked Sung-mi.

"I'm on the Board of Directors -- my family's been part of the East India Airship Line since it was just a subsidiary of the East India Company itself."

"And the obfuscation?"

"Because it's none of your damned business," he groused. "This is proprietary technology -- the future of air travel. And it's ours! I didn't want some nosey journalist," he glared at Sung-mi, "or some professional bleeding heart," he shot a glance at Declan, "blabbing about it to the press, revealing our secrets, getting all alarmist about the *Juliet*'s misadventure, while we were still working out the kinks."

"Kinks?" demanded Sung-mi. "The public has a right to know if these vessels aren't safe."

"Of course they're safe," he growled. Then he stopped, slightly chagrined. "I mean, we're still airborne, aren't we?" he finished lamely.

"It wasn't just about proprietary technology, though, was it?" prodded Declan. "It was about averting scandal."

"Of course it's about averting scandal!" He flung up his hands. "Everywhere you turn there're rabble rousers ready with pickets. The same animal rights nutters who got us to take the bonobos off ships would have a field day if they found out we were experimenting with animal brains on the bridge. The bloody socialists would start picketing if they knew we were planning on replacing the bridge crews. Passengers complain about ticket prices, but everything we do to cut costs has someone complaining its immoral or unethical or unsustainable."

"It's getting so you can't get rich without someone asking about the cost," Declan said dryly.

"Precisely," Sir Marshall agreed.

"There's *something* on that island," Percival said quietly. They turned to see the hulking purser standing before the glass, squinting. Surprised, they followed his gaze but his eyesight was markedly keener than theirs.

Sung-mi spied heavy binoculars hanging from a hook and grabbed them. Rolling the focus she peered at the approaching shore. "It's partially hidden by the curve of the shore." She handed the binoculars to Declan. "I can't make it out."

The *Romeo* hungrily consumed the distance between them and the island as Declan adjusted the focus. "It looks like -- it's a wreck of some sort. A sea vessel. No. An airship! It's smashed to pieces but the lines look familiar." Then he recalled where he had seen a similar vessel: it was when he had boarded the *Romeo*. "I think it's the *Juliet!*"

Sung-mi turned accusingly upon Sir Marshall. "How is that possible? She hasn't been put into service since she came back from..." Her words drifted off. "She never came back -- did she? That was all a lie."

Sir Marshall shifted uncomfortably. Then he squared his shoulders defiantly. "We assumed she'd been lost in a storm. So we sent out a release saying she needed a refit, so the press wouldn't be asking why she wasn't in service. It was just a test cruise -- no passengers, and a skeleton crew. Easy enough to bury the details. I mean, we just assumed it was a freak mishap -- no reason to ground the *Romeo* over a mishap, was there?" he demanded, as if they couldn't help but see his point of view.

"We'll see if my readers -- and the aviation regulatory board -- agree when we get back," Sung-mi said tartly. Then, grimly, she added: "*If* we get back." She turned to Declan. "Any indication of survivors?" But she knew the answer. The *Juliet* had vanished a few weeks ago, and the island appeared conspicuously barren of edible food or fresh water. Assuming anyone survived the crash itself. "How did it crash?" she asked. "I thought these ships used helium?"

"It doesn't look like an explosion," Declan muttered, still peering through the binoculars. "More like it was deliberately scuttled. They could have voided gas from the balloon until she was too heavy to stay aloft."

"Why would they do that?"

"Perhaps *they* didn't," said Pericles softly. "My eyes are not as acute as they used to be, but have you identified what surrounds the wreck?"

Pericles was being overly modest, Declan thought as he rolled the focus again, trying to make out what it was that had caught the purser's attention. There were strange growths covering the basalt ground, mostly white or yellow-white, as if long bleached by the sun. Some appeared almost like massive logs of driftwood, though given the island's absence of flora it was unclear from whence they could have come. Other protuberances arced up like the finger bones of giants, frozen as they clutched futilely for the heavens. Gradually he recognized what he was observing. Vertebrae. Ribs. "The shore is carpeted with hundreds of...bones!" he breathed at last.

"The dead crew?"

He shook his head. "Much bigger. Almost like," he hesitated, his words racing faster than his thoughts, "like the bones of whales."

"An elephants' graveyard," muttered Sir Marshall. "In Africa I heard rumours of places where elephants go to die. Never saw proof of it myself, though."

"A whales' graveyard?" said Sung-mi, incredulous. "In the middle of nowhere? But why would the *Juliet*-?" She stopped, putting a hand to her mouth in horror. "Its brain had been scooped out of its body, plugged into this cold machine. It -- it just wanted to die. But why did the *Romeo* come looking? That screaming before -- was it calling for the *Juliet*?" Even more aghast she looked at Sir Marshall. "Why were the ship's named the *Romeo* and the *Juliet*?"

The older man stubbornly refused to meet her gaze. "I think I heard something about the whaling vessel that caught them finding them together," he admitted grudgingly.

"The problem is," Declan said, lowering the binoculars, and realizing how absurd that sounded -- as if their problems could be reduced to just one, "those don't quite resemble whale bones." He turned on Sir Marshall. "Just what were these creatures?"

"Whales," he insisted. Then he shrugged. "I mean, I assume. We commissioned a whaling vessel to get us a couple of whale brains -- outfitted her with tanks, instructed the crew in how to administer the nutrients, keep the brains alive. After a few months, the vessel came chugging back into port with these. I think there was something in the confidential shareholders' memo about the whaler captain saying they were odd-looking beasties though."

"So you outsourced the brain-harvesting to a whaler who sailed out to the deepest part of the ocean, where any recognizable whale he'd want to keep for himself for its oils and blubber and meat, and instead he scooped the brains out of God-knows-what he hauled out of the ocean's depths? Is that a fair assessment of the situation-?" Declan stopped as something else caught his eye. He raised the binoculars again, though by now they were close enough that he scarcely needed them.

Peering past his shoulder, Sung-mi whispered, "What is *that*?"

There was a formation among the black craggy cliffs of the nameless island; a weird outcropping of rock that it seemed impossible could have been formed by nature alone. Stone tendrils reached up toward the sky, for all the world like some nameless artisan had carved the arms of an octopus from the rock. As the island neared, they could distinguish a deeper blackness in the rock beneath the stone tentacles -- an aperture of some sort, as though the entrance to a cave, or a-

"Temple," Declan breathed through clenched teeth. "An Elder God temple."

"I've heard of those," Sung-mi admitted. "Ancient ruins have been uncovered in recent years -- often attracting neo-cultists. But surely this island was never capable of supporting human life?"

"No one has proven definitively that such temples were built by humans," Declan said tightly, lowering the binoculars. "Pericles -- commence the evacuation, please."

"Yes, sir," the giant purser said matter-of-factly, unhooking a speaking tube and blowing into it. After a moment he said, "Mr. Jenkins, begin an orderly disembarkation, if you please. Yes -- crew as well as passengers."

"Steady on," objected Sir Marshall. "Don't get your knickers in a knot over some blasted *National Geographic* photo-spread."

Declan turned on him. Even shielded by his snow goggles his glare was palpable. "There are still presences in this world man does not fully understand. I've encountered similar ruins in my travels -- it tends to end rather badly." He shot a glance at the disembodied brain, culled from God-only-knew what manner of creature that called the ocean depths home and which was compulsively driven to lay its bones at the doorstep of this ancient temple. "Besides, if the *Romeo* intends to crash itself next to the *Juliet* -- we don't want to be aboard her when she does. And we don't want to be marooned on *that* island."

Sir Marshall's shoulders slumped. "Very well. Boy -- uh, purser -- go make sure they're holding a boat for us. Wouldn't want to get left behind, what?"

"Of course, sir." The hulking Sasquatch lumbered quickly from the bridge.

"We'd best follow," Declan said tersely. He draped an arm almost possessively around Sung-mi and herded her toward the exit. As they came abreast of Sir Marshal there was a hiss of releasing steam and his mechanical arm flashed out with the near-invisible speed of a mousetrap snapping closed.

It would have taken Declan's head off. But Declan was already ducking, and with his arm about Sung-mi, had shoved her out of harm's way. He wheeled to face the older man.

"Yes, well -- very good," Sir Marshall said grudgingly, smoothing his mutton chops with his flesh hand. "Very astute of you. You appreciate my predicament, then, yes? I mean, the company has made some poor decisions -- I won't deny it. The cost-cutting, the experimental technology, the cover-up of the *Juliet*. And rest assured, heads will roll. But damn it, man, if all this came out, stock would sink lower than Davey Jones' and all that. I'd be nigh ruined. As it is, I think this can be presented as an unfortunate misadventure -- storm damage, don't you know, and, uh, human error. The crew and the passengers don't know anything about what's really occurred, after all. As long as you two aren't around to go blabbing to the gutter press."

"Pericles-" began Sung-mi.

"He'll keep a still tongue in his head if he wants his job. And even if he doesn't -- he's a 'squatch. What's his word worth, hmm? But *you* two? You're a tad more problematic."

Keeping himself between Sir Marshall and Sung-mi, Declan said tightly, "This is madness. Look out the window." The black, craggy cliffs now overwhelmed the vista from one side of the bridge to the other. "You don't want to be on board when she crashes."

"All the more reason to finish this quickly, don't you think?" He charged at Declan, his mechanical arm wheezing as the powerful pistons pumped eagerly away. The younger man made to shield Sung-mi -- only to discover she was no longer beside him. He leapt away as Sir Marshall's iron fist tore a ragged gash in the wall behind where he'd been standing. He then stepped in and delivered an upper cut to the older man's side. But whatever could be said about Sir Marshall's character, his physique had clearly benefitted from all those safari hunts. He grunted but didn't fall. His mechanical arm snapped back, glancing off Declan's head, sending the already bandaged man reeling away. Sir Marshall charged at him again -- then halted in mid-stride. Sung-mi was by one wall, fiddling with loose wires that, if his memory served, the Sasquatch purser had earlier yanked out. "Just what are you up to, young la-"

That hellish screaming flooded the air once more as Sung-mi succeeded in reattaching the sound system wires. The older man doubled over, clutching his ears. Declan, though, was better braced for the cacophonous assault having deduced Sung-mi's intent. He tackled Sir Marshall, sending the older man slamming against the brain's tank. He reached over and yanked Sung-mi to her feet, the woman having crumpled from the aural bombardment. Together they raced from the room.

They stumbled through the deserted airship, the siren-scream, so horrific and yet so poignant, seeming almost to have a physical presence, buffeting them like a gale wind. Suddenly Pericles loomed before them, his massive hands clapped to his ears. "Sir? Madam? I heard the screaming resume and came to see-!"

"The escape boats!" shouted Declan.

"Of course!" the purser yelled back, wheeling about and leading them toward the vessel's hangar. "Sir Marshall?"

"Has elected to go down with the ship!"

If that statement gave the purser any pause, he remained unflappable. "Very good, sir."

They raced into the low-ceilinged hanger, the far wall gaping open so that wind slapped them about and the vast, depthless sea spread before them. Pericles ushered them into the only remaining life boat and kicked off from the deck.

The boat slid out the opening and plunged into empty air. Sung-mi clutched Declan's arm and Declan knotted his fists about the restraining bar as the drop in altitude sent a rush from his groin to his head. They heard a crackle of unfurling canvas as the kite automatically deployed on its tether. The boat jerked, sending all three doubling over, then continued to drop but at a much reduced speed. As they fell Declan spied the other life boats already upon the ocean, their kites dragging them further out to sea. Then they hit the water with a thud that he felt in his kidneys, spewing brine over them.

As one, all three turned to watch the mammoth hulk of the *Romeo* barrelling toward the shore, noticeably shedding altitude as the undead brain sought to join its mate -- its *Juliet* -- in death, amid the bones of its people at the foot of a temple erected to nameless gods.

It was both heart-breaking -- and deeply unsettling.

He stirred, realizing Pericles was speaking.

"..equipped with food and water supplies. Plus a compass and nautical map," he was explaining, gesturing at stout cabinets in the life boat. "With luck, we should be able to navigate to more frequently travelled sea lanes-"

They jumped as the thunderous crash of the *Romeo* echoed across the swells.

"May God have mercy on him," muttered Sung-mi.

"Sir Marshall?"

She looked at him. "Oh -- him, too." Then she smiled weakly. "Your bandages have come loose." Embarrassed, Declan hastily reached to reset them -- but a delicate hand on his arm stopped him. "No -- it's okay. It looks as though the skin has started to heal. Some good news in the end."

He gave her a half-smile, then looked back toward the shrinking island as their kite pulled them further and further away.

D.K. Latta *has been writing fiction, mostly of the speculative fiction variety, off and on for over two decades, as well as occasional non-fiction reviews and essays about movies, graphic novels, and pop culture. He lives in Canada.*

Sea Change
E.M. Anderson

Storms come fast to the island.

Breakers hammer the shore, thundering up the beach like hippocampi. Palms sway. The sea roils, slate-gray all the way to the horizon. Black clouds billow through the sky, tripping over each other in their haste to make land.

Mab stands in the doorway, a hand on the lintel. Queen Mab, I call her. She isn't beautiful, maybe never was. Short and wiry, with cordy arms and a hawkish nose that's been broken at least twice. Thick silver braid, long and coarse. Skin leathery and brown from salt and sun after three decades in paradise, as she calls it dryly. Clad in shirt and trousers carefully patched and mended and repatched and re-mended.

But her eyes are the color of the ocean at dawn.

She squints at the thrashing sea as I stumble toward the shack. Sand bites my legs, blown from the dunes by the howling wind.

"Storm coming in," I spit out.

She snorts, moving aside. "I got eyes, boy."

I slink past. I don't know why I speak to her. More often than not, I get this, a snort and a derisive comment.

But she's my only company—I hers, rather, since she's been marooned here long before the shipwreck that left my crewmates dead. Long before I was even born. And she has those ocean-dawn eyes.

I keep thinking maybe one day she'll think something of me. Six months on this godforsaken spit of land, and so far, she thinks me a child. A boy of barely twenty winters, foolish enough to leave a life of comfort for a life at sea. The queen jeers at my choices, my fresh face—impossibly young no matter how weathered it gets, irritatingly beardless no matter how long I leave off shaving—my short career as a sailor, the tragedy of my shipwreck, destroyed by a storm like this one.

Still I try to win her approval. She isn't pleasant company, but she's company—and all that stands between me and death.

When I first recovered, trying to help in repayment for her care, I all but killed us three different ways. First with wood I'd chopped, which had already burned my skin, its sap flying from the ax to bite my hands and arms; Mab disposed of it, calm but surly, explaining manchineel wood could not be safely burned. Then with fruit I'd collected from the same: small, sweet-smelling things like crabapples, which Mab again disposed of, less calm, more surly, explaining the fruit would kill us if we ate more than a bite. At last with leaves I'd collected, again from the same, thinking to use them in the water-closet, or rather the latrine several dozen yards from both our shack and our water supply. With no calm whatsoever and all the surl she could muster (a great deal), Mab told me in exceedingly crude language what I could expect to happen if I used the leaves as intended and stalked off.

"Fifty different trees on this island," she snapped, "and you *will* use the one meant to kill us."

She might've let me kill myself through my own ineptitude; I own it would've saved her a great deal of trouble. Instead, she tended my burns from the murderous plant, more gently than I expected, and has been my teacher these six months since.

When she stands in the doorway like this, watching a rising storm, I feel with uneasy certainty that she's taught me to survive because she knows she must leave me one day to do so alone. The roiling clouds reflect in her ocean eyes. The waves roar on the beach. The wind rips through the shack, rustling the books on Mab's desk, both of which, books and desk, come from God knows where, are an eternal source of mystery to me.

As is her fascination with storms.

I shiver, swallowing my unease because she'll only mock me for it. "Will you not close the door? This storm is like every other."

She shakes her head. "Could be different. Could be her."

Her voice is softer than I've ever heard it. My insides prickle.

"Her who?"

She half turns, raising an eyebrow. "Ain't I ever told you the tale of Admete?"

Mocking, as usual, everything she says caustic like she can't help herself, but there's that softness again, curling around *Admete* like a lover's caress. Admete, Greek: *undefeated,* if the recollection of my boyish book-learning is worth anything. Unbroken. Untamed.

Mab closes the door. Blessed relief. The wind howls around the shack, but the pages still and the storm seems suddenly distant. The shack is warm and dim, lit only by a fire Mab keeps burning noon and night against the power of the wild expanse outside.

Mab sits beside the fire—on the floor, but it might as well be a throne. She leans back on her elbows, legs stretched before her, gnarled head thrown back. She isn't beautiful, maybe never was, but lounging on the floor this way, face in profile, gilded in the firelight, she seems an ancient, eldritch goddess of the sea.

"A daughter of the ocean, she is," Mab murmurs. The words mean nothing, but her tone is waves lapping the shore on a still day at sunset. "The wind, the breakers, the wild gales, all of 'em, it's her. *Beware Admete,* the other sailors'd tell me, *beware the wild sea-maiden. She'll run you aground sure as you're born.*

"I liked the sound of that, I thought, some maiden puttin' the fear a God into all them sailors. Used to pray to her, of sorts. Every time we went out, I'd say, *Admete, if it please you, bring me'n'all these bonehead sailors back safe*. And every time we come in, I'd say, '*Til we meet again, Admete, thank ye*. Started talking to her on voyages, too. Thought of her as the sea itself, the sea turned human."

Mab leans forward, drawn toward the fire like tides to the shore. Her eyes dance, alive with the reflection of the flames and the memory of Admete.

"So happens it was me crew I had to watch, not Admete," she says. "They never did like a woman captaining 'em. Bad luck, so they said, and every time they did I'd point at the water and say, *There's the door, then*, and a course they'd never leave on account of us being in the middle of the ocean and them needing a ship and a captain.

"But at last the day come when they mutinied. Come at me when I was sleeping—course they did, knew as well's I did they'd never get the jump on me if I were awake. Woke up already half-bound. Fought with might and main, I did, and more'n one of 'em's bleedin' by the time they get the job done.

"But they get me out on deck and're ready to toss me clean overboard, only they want to make a to-do of it, see, do it proper, so they start recitin' all the wrongs I done 'em and their rights as sailors.

"Well, a storm come up from nowhere as they finished their ganchin'. Worst storm I ever seen, and I'd seen my share, some ten years at sea. The wind howled gleeful-like, ripped the mast clean down—sails first, then the whole thing, with a creak and a crack and a groan like a tree. The waves leapt so high they fair swallowed us, one after another rollin' right over the deck. Not a man could stay on his feet more than a moment.

"Then lightning come forkin' down right onto the ship, crackin' and sizzlin', and blew a hole in the hull. Hit the armory, it did, bust up all the gunpowder.

"They really start panicking then, and one of 'em grabs me and throws me over. I'm coughin' and chokin', and I'm still bound up, and the rope's swellin' with water. And the ship's sinkin' faster than I ever seen, all afire now and groaning like anything, and my treacherous crew goin' down with it because they know there's no use jumpin' for it, 'cuz the swirlin' water'll suck 'em right down with the ship. And I can't swim, and I'm dead for sure, and I know it, and it almost don't matter that they mutinied, 'cuz with a storm like this, I'm dead either way."

Outside, the storm picks up, same as it does in Mab's story. Wind howling, thunder roaring, or maybe it's the breakers, crashing so wild I can hear them all the way up here. The shack trembles.

Mab gazes into the fire without noticing. For all her talk of that long-ago storm, her face is soft.

"Washed up on the beach," she says, "just as gently as if I'd been carried there. And when I come to, she was there. Admete."

Her ocean eyes are distant. Her tone is gentle, but it disconcerts me. Mab is not gentle. Mab is not distant. Mab is acerbic and practical and endlessly present, thinking nothing of past or future except when she tells her stories.

I've never seen her roam so far in her storytelling. And as she watches the fire and dreams of Admete, her faraway look—the same one she wears when she watches storms—makes me feel with dread certainty that I'll lose her one day.

Her finger traces circles on the floor beside her. "She was the most beautiful woman I'd ever seen. Hair like night, eyes like the sun but wilder, voice that'd make you run your own ship aground tryin' to reach her. And she smelled like the sea, and her skin was soft and smooth as seaglass."

My insides prickle again. Her finger's travel over the floor slows, gentles, like she's remembering touching that soft, smooth skin. But she's a mother's age, older, a grandmother's, so I look away and clench myself against the prickling.

"She saved me," Mab says. "'Twas her, that storm. She saw my crew turn on me and saved me. Heard my prayers all those years, she said. No one'd ever prayed to her before but me."

Admete tended Mab's wounds, but she stayed on the island long after they were healed. Mab has told me crude stories before, cackling like a witch when I blush, and I think I'm prepared to listen to graphically detailed memories of her body tangled with the sea-maiden's. Instead, each time she approaches the topic, she falls silent, her finger circling slower and slower on the floor, like their lovemaking was sacred, too precious to put to words.

It embarrasses me far more than her crudity. Like I'm intruding on them in memory, seeing something too private to ever have been intended for me. My fingers dig into my knees.

Mab is quiet, and I can't stand what I'm sure she's remembering, so I break the silence bluntly.

"What happened to her?"

Mab rouses herself. "Eh?"

Rain seeps in, dripping into the fire. The flames hiss.

"She's not here." I clench my fists. "Admete."

Her name is poison on my tongue.

Mab hunches, running a hand through her hair. "She went back."

"Back?"

"To the sea. More'n a year with me, must a been, when she walked right into the water. Vanished like foam."

Mab's every line is weary, defeated, in a way I've never seen. "Can't be on land too long, she told me. I could see it in her. She'd started fading, wilting like a flower. But she promised she'd return to me."

The fire crackles and pops.

"She promised," Mab repeats.

The prickling claws at me like a sea-bird's talons. It digs into me, this dread that Mab will leave me, because now I know why.

The wind roars. The shack quakes. Mab raises her head, her ocean eyes narrowed at the door like she's heard someone knocking. Defeat sharpens to vigilance; she's alert as a pointer dog.

"It's a storm," I say. "Nothing more."

She rises in one fluid motion. "Storms are hers."

She strides to the door, flings it open. The storm is inside, wind whipping through the shack, throwing books and papers across the room. The fire flares, roars, leaps from its pit to devour the flying pages.

"Mab!" I cry, but she's already outside, so I scramble to my feet and follow.

Rain stings my face. I stagger over the dunes after my sea-queen, wind pushing me sideways and backways and every which way but after Mab.

She's impervious, as she always is, always has been, to everything. Everything except the memory of Admete.

She walks strong and sure, bare feet sinking into sand as she strides toward the angry ocean.

"Admete!" Her voice is the yearning lament of a gull. "Addie, love. I beg ye."

"*Mab!*" I scream.

She stops.

Her chest heaves. She's ankle-deep in water. Each crashing wave sprays her with salt, but she squints into it with an expression so hopeful it pains me. I struggle toward her, fighting this wind that won't let me follow.

"Addie," she calls again in that gull-voice. "Addie, please. You said you'd come for me."

In the breakers, a flicker. A form.

I freeze. My heart pounds. My eyes are bewitched, surely, a trick of the wind and rain and my own dread, but I see, out in the waves, the shape of a woman.

"Admete," Mab breathes.

My heart stops. Sand sucks at my feet like sludge.

"Mab," I whisper, "don't," but the spectral form opens her arms, and Mab walks into the sea.

Lightning forks across the sky, striking so close I smell the sizzle. Stars burst before my eyes. By the time I can see again, both women are gone, and I'm alone except for a gull streaking improbably across the stormy sky. Then the gull is gone, too, lost beyond the clouds, like Mab is lost, like I'm lost, frozen in the sand, alone on this godforsaken spit of land my sea-queen called paradise, with the wind howling in triumph and the ocean surging up the beach to claim me.

E.M. Anderson (she/her) is a queer, neurodivergent writer. Her work has appeared in Wizards in Space, Dark Horses: The Magazine of Weird Fiction, and SJ Whitby's Awakenings: A Cute Mutants Anthology. Her debut novel, The Remarkable Retirement of Edna Fisher, is forthcoming from Hansen House Books in April 2023.

At Dragonbone Bay
Hesper Leveret

Voltaea kept trying to see what lay ahead, but they were sailing into the sun, and the light reflected off the water's surface was so bright it left her completely dazzled. If she turned around, however, and looked at what lay behind, the water was so clear she could see all the way down. The rocky seabed looked almost close enough to touch. And then a shark swam beneath their small boat, and she had a sudden sense of vertigo as she realised those rocks were seventeen fathoms below her, and that what she had taken for a pebble was a boulder large enough to hide a giant octopus.

A pod of dolphins raced past, leaping out of the water and clicking to each other. Voltaea felt envious of their speed; without much of a breeze, their small lateen-rigged sail hung mostly limp. And of course she wasn't entitled to command the royal wind mages. Yet.

She thought of the shell-shard crown which would soon be hers. If she could prove her bravery and ruthlessness to her mother - and none of her cousins succeeded in usurping her rightful place as the heir to the Fisher Kingdom. She could picture the circlet of gleaming white shards, and imagine the weight of it on her head, how it would feel to wear it and command the obedience of teeming multitudes.

'Stop thinking about the crown,' said Anseen, her bloodbound guard and sole companion on this day, without breaking the rhythm of his oar strokes. The tattoos on his bare arms and chest rippled as he rowed, their swirling patterns mimicking the motion of the sea. The patterns continued onto her own arms in a single design, as befitted their blood bond.

'I wasn't,' lied Voltaea, and Anseen gave a roll of his eyes which was so small it would have been imperceptible to anyone but her. Voltaea made a tiny, unnecessary adjustment to the rudder as an excuse for not paying him any attention for a moment. 'And how could you tell, anyway?' she asked.

'You get this look when you're thinking about it,' he said. 'Like you're enjoying being superior to everyone else.'

'But I...' There wasn't really a good way to end that sentence. Voltaea tried something else. 'How exactly is this little voyage supposed to help me, anyway? While I'm away, my cousins could be trying anything. And it's just Dragonbone Bay. I've seen dead dragons before, you know.'

'I know. But you haven't seen the Queen.'

'And you think me seeing this Queen will help make me Queen?'

'Yes,' said Anseen.

'How?'

In response, Anseen just said the Words from the Deep. 'The salt water flows through our veins, and teaches us the wisdom of the sea. We learn to be as patient as the whale, as fierce and focused as the shark, as ingenious as the octopus, as sociable as the sardine, as kind as the oyster.'

Voltaea sighed. As ever, Anseen resorted to quoting empty snippets of wisdom at her when he couldn't – or wouldn't – provide her with actual answers. He could be infuriating sometimes. And besides - were whales really that patient? Or just very large? And were oysters actually kind – or did they not make their pearls as gifts for the Fisher Kingdom at all, but for their own purposes? As for the social spirit of the sardine, that was the stupidest one of all, since it just made them easier to catch in large numbers.

Octopuses were ingenious, though. And sharks were certainly fierce and focused. She'd give him that.

As they carried on, further into Dragonbone Bay, she started to see the fossils that gave this place its name. Scattered bones at first, standing out dark against the greyish-blue rocks, and then complete skeletons, as big as humpback whales. The curved rows of vertebrae finishing at one end in a spiked tail, and at the other in a grinning, sharp-toothed skull. The rib cages, housing whole colonies of sea creatures. The wingbones, delicate in comparison with the ribs, though still massive. Sometimes these were spread out to either side of the body; other times, they were tucked in close. The bodies were usually found alone. Sometimes there would be a smaller skeleton alongside – a dragon child, Voltaea assumed. As usual, the sight of these long-dead leviathans of the air resting under the water sent a shiver down her spine. What had killed them? Why had so many fallen here? The answers were long since lost – if, indeed, they had ever been known.

Eventually, Anseen stopped rowing, wiped the sweat from his brow, and let the boat simply drift on the current for a few moments. 'We're nearly at the Queen,' he said.

'I can't see anything,' said Voltaea, squinting against the sun. And then she looked straight down, and she saw.

The tip of the tail, beneath the boat and as big as the boat. The tail itself, curving across the seabed, each vertebra the size of a tiger shark, and getting bigger the closer they were to the body. Voltaea's mind drew back from the sight, refusing to process what she was seeing. Nothing could be that size. Nothing that had ever been alive could have grown that big, with wings that would blot out the sun over an entire city, and a rib cage that could contain her mother's palace, several times over. As they floated over that rib cage, the tallest ribs were in danger of grazing the underside of the boat. Inside, a whole forest of red kelp had grown up, some strands of it breaking the surface.

The neck was curled round, the head facing backwards, as if the creature had died in pain, although what could cause pain to something of that size, Voltaea didn't want to imagine. The mighty skull was big enough that her mother's flagship could have sailed right through its jaws, and its empty eye sockets stared up at her, two great pools of darkness.

Voltaea drew in her breath, and pulled her eyes away from the scene beneath the waves, refocusing on the boat itself, and on Anseen. Even though she knew the creature had been dead for centuries, or even millennia, she somehow felt that if she kept on looking at it, she would see it see it start to move, stirring from the seabed and rising up to the surface to take flight again on its skeletal wings, skimming over the sea, opening its mouth to swallow all the ships of the Fisher Kingdom.

Anseen smiled at her. 'That's the Queen.'

Voltaea let her breath out again, slowly and deliberately. 'Well, I guess I've seen her now.'

Anseen kept smiling. She hated it when he did that. 'You haven't seen her heart.'

'Her heart?'

'The size of a house, and calcified over the centuries, until it resembles a huge broken pearl.'

'How do you know? Have you seen it?'

'I have seen shards of it. And so have you.'

It took her a moment to understand, while his smile grew wider. 'The crown,' she breathed.

'The very same,' he said, and then his smile abruptly vanished. 'The tradition – passed down from generation to generation – is that every heir to the throne of the Fisher Kingdom must dive to the heart of the dragon queen, and break off a fresh shard to add to the crown.'

'What? You're joking!'

He shook his head, his face now grave.

'Then why have I never heard of this tradition before now?'

'Because it's a secret, kept by the bloodbound guard to the queen's eldest daughter, until such time as he deems her ready to attempt the dive.'

'And you think I'm ready now?'

In answer, Anseen simply inclined his head towards the water, and pulled on the oars to hold the boat in position. Voltaea felt another shiver go through her. She was an experienced diver – obviously, she was the eldest daughter of the queen, she'd been swimming and diving since before she could even walk – but the thought of plunging down towards that mighty skeleton horrified her in a way she couldn't quite articulate, even to herself.

'Do my cousins know about this?'

Anseen shook his head. 'Not yet. They'll find out only if you fail.'

'If I fail? How many attempts do I get?'

Anseen actually laughed at that.

'All right,' said Voltaea, and filled her lungs. Better to get it over with, before she could scare herself with nameless terrors and lose her chance at the shell-shard crown. She pulled off her loose tunic and slipped over the side of the boat, in a single fluid motion.

Wearing only a knife strapped to her thigh, she swam rapidly downwards, heading for the centre of the rib-cage and the red kelp forest within. Anseen had positioned the boat as closely as he could to the middle of the queen's gigantic torso, although he couldn't know for sure where the heart itself was located, and the kelp forest would make it harder to find. She needed to get down there fast, and start her search - with only a single lungful of air, every second would count. Soon, she was between the ribs, and the long strands of kelp rose up around her. She kept going. As she went deeper, the water cooled down, going from blood-warm to a chill against her bare skin. This was as deep as she had ever been, as deep as the divers of the Fisher Kingdom ever went in their hunt for pearls and corals and sponges. But she could go deeper – she knew she could.

Once she was in the middle of the kelp, she could no longer see the skeleton, and so she could forget for the moment about its intimidating size, and tell herself that this wasn't a dive to retrieve a shard from the heart of a long-dead dragon; it was just another pearl dive.

Then she saw the heart. She needn't have worried about not being able to find it; it was so big, and so beautifully lustrous, gleaming amidst the crimson fronds. It would have taken her breath away, only she was far too well trained to waste oxygen at a time like this.

Voltaea swam towards it, and reached for her knife. She rapidly tried to figure out where was the weakest point, the place where she could most easily break off a shard. It was already broken around the top, where others had taken shards before her, and the seabed around it was littered with what she took for pieces of calcified arteries – similar to the heart, though without its lustre. The way it was broken made her feel strangely sad; surely, she thought, it would have been better to keep the heart whole, and send a whole team of divers to retrieve it and carry it back to the palace? Maybe once she was Queen of the Fisher Kingdom, she could order it done, even repair the heart, restore the lost shards to their rightful place...

The lost shards? The shards, that is, that made up the crown, the very crown she had so long coveted and dreamt of? The shards which would represent her authority? Including the shard she needed to retrieve right now, if she ever wanted to become heir, let alone queen? Voltaea dismissed such thoughts, and turned to the task at hand. She spotted a likely-looking place, where a thin, jagged edge stuck out, and set to work with the serrated edge of her blade.

Her foot came to rest on the uneven seabed, and crunched against something. One of the calcified arteries. Then Voltaea glanced down, and saw that it wasn't a dragon artery at all. It was a bone – a human bone. And the rest of the skeleton lay nearby, scattered slightly by the marine scavengers which had picked it clean. It must be an unsuccessful predecessor, a previous royal hopeful who had failed to retrieve a shard of her own.

Except – there were too many bones, for this to be just one person. Far too many, all around the heart. This was a human graveyard, inside a dragon's skeleton. There must be dozens of people here, all lying dead at the bottom of Dragonbone Bay, drowned in the attempt to claim the crown. Voltaea didn't know if the dragon queen had taken any human lives while she was alive, but she had certainly killed many since she had died, all of them – she assumed – members of the royal family. Her family.

And it was that thought, more than the simple presence of the bones, that made her lose concentration at her task, and caused her hand to slip. The knife skidded off the hard surface of the heart, and cut deep into the skin of her wrist. Blood bloomed in the water.

Voltaea let out an involuntary gasp of pain, and with it went some of her precious air. She was in trouble now – her lungs starting to burn, and her blood was scenting the water. There were always sharks in Dragonbone Bay, and surrounded by the red kelp, she wouldn't see one approach until it was nearly upon her. She had to work fast, get her shard, and get back to the surface.

Or – did she have to do all that? Voltaea knew she had no time to think, and yet think she did. She had coveted the shell-shard crown all her life, longed to rule the Fisher Kingdom, and now she had discovered that the crown was made not from shell at all, but from pieces of the heart of a long-dead creature of the air. A dragon queen, who had claimed the lives of many who had gone before her, and all for what? A stolen piece of a calcified heart? How did that prove anyone worthy of ruling over the pearl divers, the fishermen, the seaweed farmers, all those who followed the words from the deep and the wisdom of the sea?

Voltaea made her decision, and turned her face back towards the surface, where she could see the boat, so far above her it looked tiny and insignificant, no bigger than a shark swimming far away. She kicked off from the seabed, disturbing the bones, and swam rapidly upwards, leaving a trail of blood behind her. She knew she would pay later for this too-fast ascent, but she didn't have any time to lose. She needed more air, before she did what she had to do next.

Her head broke the surface, and she took a huge, gulping breath, before grabbing hold of the side of the boat and throwing herself inside. Seeing her arrive with nothing except her knife, Anseen frowned in disappointment.

'You didn't do it,' he said. 'I was sure you could do it. And – you're bleeding. What happened down there?'

Voltaea gasped a few more breaths, and then answered him.

'I decided I don't want the shell-shard crown.'

'What? But your whole life-'

'My whole life I've wanted my mother's crown. Now I've changed my mind. I don't want my mother's crown any more. I want my own.'

'Your own crown?'

'That's right,' said Voltaea. She tore a strip from her tunic and bound it round her wrist.

'You know I can't let you dive again and make another attempt at the heart,' he said. 'My honour as a bloodbound guard...'

'Will remain intact. I don't intend to dive for the heart again. I don't want a crown made of bits of dead dragon. I want a crown made of something to represent the Fisher Kingdom, and the wisdom of the sea. To represent me.'

Anseen raised his eyebrows. The beginnings of a smile tugged at the corners of his mouth. 'Like what?'

Voltaea looked over his shoulder, where she could see a fin cutting through the water, close to where she had swum to the surface. A large fin. That would do. She bared her teeth at him in a broad grin. 'As fierce and focused as the shark,' she said, and grabbed her knife. Then she jumped over the side of the boat, to claim her own crown. A crown made of shark's teeth.

Hesper Leveret *is a speculative fiction writer based in Liverpool, UK. Her work has previously appeared in Fireside, Luna Station Quarterly, and the 'Prismatic Dreams' anthology from All Worlds Wayfarer, and is forthcoming in Interzone.*

A Song for the Dregs
Brian Maycock

After he was made redundant from the textile mill my dad became a siren.

We lived on the outskirts of Manchester at the time. There were three of us in the family, which made us stand out on our street where all the other terraces had at least four children crammed into them.

As an only child I was a freak as far as the rest of the kids were concerned. None of them cared why I was different as they called me names and kicked me.

The truth was that after I was born my mum was told by a doctor not to have any more children. Carrying me to term almost killed her.

She told me this once when she had a drink in her, and I often thought afterwards that I deserved the boot-marks which stained my skin.

When I found out my dad was leaving, life got even worse.

I was sixteen years old, and I learnt he was going when I overheard him and Mum in their room arguing.

"What else do you expect me to do! I need to earn a wage and there's nothing round here," he said to her, his voice raised, but held back enough for the words to not bleed through the paper-thin walls to next door and the eager ears waiting there.

"What will people say when they find out you've left me?" Mum spat out.

"Tell them I'm working on the docks, offloading the ships. Tell them the truth," he jabbed back.

Mum was not having it. "They'll never believe it. And I certainly don't. Everyone knows you're shiftless, a big, lazy bag of bile, and that's why you got fired. No one else got

73

laid off from the mill. Not even Charlie Winters and he's regular down with the Gripe. So don't talk to me about the truth, not when you're tossing a bucket of lies in my face."

Dad's only comeback was to slam the door and walk out into the street.

The bus stop was right outside our front door, so he had no choice but to stand there for thirty minutes, the suitcase by his ankles speaking volumes, while a ripple of twitching net curtains flowed up and down the street, and mum gulped sherry.

"He's dead to me," she kept saying, then refilled her glass. "Dead and buried."

I left her to her mourning of the man she could see through the window scratching his backside and went out the back door.

I was close to tears.

Not only was I an only child, now I was half an orphan.

My dad had sliced himself away from us and surely the bullies would swarm around me worse than ever now.

Unlike the prophecies in the Bible that were dangled in front of us at Sunday School but never happened, my prophecy came to pass straight away.

The bus with my dad on was only just slipping out of view when Tom Mitchell and his twin, Meg, came sauntering down the alley where I was trying to push tears back into my eyes and sideways off my cheeks.

"You've got no, Pa," Tom spat out.

Meg chimed in: "No Pa, and your Ma's going to marry the man in the moon and then she'll go away too."

"You'll be all alone and you'll smell of poo," Tom finished then grinned wickedly and I knew exactly what was coming.

His boot rushed up towards my chin, and my teeth slammed together, against each other. I winced. My tongue, caught in the middle, burnt with pain.

"He's coming back," I claimed. Which earned me a kick on the shin from Meg.

More kids appeared.

In no time at all, I was in the eye of a snot-rich storm. Having nostrils fired at me was new but did not distract from the pain of all those toes clenched tight inside leather.

I was left crawling away once supper had been called from open windows and made my way back inside to find my mum, her head tipped back, her mouth wide open, dribble trailing down her chin and a snore grinding through her nose.

I wiped as much blood off me as I could using the curtains then went to bed.

The next day I woke crusted to the sheets with the blood I had missed, and hell was unleashed the moment I stepped outside.

I lasted a month and knew I could last no more.

So, I made a vow:

I would go find my dad and bring him back.

It was simple really.

I emptied the gas meter of coins, spread butter onto a heel of bread, put it in my pocket and set off walking. I had learnt from my dad's actions and was not going to catch the bus until I was well out of sight.

I was on a strange street, with strange people passing by, when I finally stepped aboard a number 23.

This was the fifth bus I had tried – the conductors on all the others had told me they did not go within a country mile of the docks.

The number 23 was the bus for me.

I settled down on a seat and ate my bread, then wiped up the butter lining my pocket with my fingers and licked them clean. This was how adventures should begin.

I smelt the docks before I saw them, the air suddenly thick with stenches I did not recognise.

These were odours so powerful I sat in a kind of daze still in my seat on the bus long after it had pulled up.

It was a new driver, getting on to take the bus back along the way, who told me to pay again or get off.

On unsteady legs and with my cheeks burning, I tottered down the aisle.

My first steps in this bizarre new land saw the rest of my senses assaulted. The sights of disfigured men, one with an arm missing, one an ear, one a nose, came at me thick and fast.

Other men brawled in the street and worse. One was bent over double, a puddle of sick spreading out in front of him, another peed on his own feet, swaying slightly as he did.

Music and laughter and bawling and cussing poured out of a building to my left.

I had learnt my letters at school and carefully turned each of the scrawls painted on the wall by its door into sounds:

T-h-e B-r-o-k-e-n A-n-c-h-o-r.

I recognised the letters for what they were but put together they made no sense to me.

I moved out of the way just in time as a new man flew spinning out of the door, to land in a heap of swearing.

After rising and brushing off his fluster, he walked away.

With no idea which direction I should be heading in, I decided to take my lead from him.

And after a dozen paces of so, decided to grab tighter onto this opportunity fate had presented to me.

"Mister," I yelled out to him, "I'm looking for my dad."

He glanced back and looked me up and down and from side to side. This took little time: I was a scrawny thing.

Then he asked, "Do you have any money?"

I brought out all my pilfered coins. They quarter-filled one palm of one of my hands.

"Can you help me find him?" I asked. "Investigate his where-he-is."

"Of course I can, son," he replied.

The smile that followed was filled with gaps and blackened stumps.

I should have known better.

But of course, I didn't.

The coins flowed from my hands into his, then disappeared into his pockets.

I waited for the search to begin.

For clues to be followed, intrigue to crackle.

Instead, he rubbed his face and said, "Mighty thirsty work this Detecting. I have been recently asked to leave The Broken Anchor and not return. I have restless debts at the High Tide Arms, and an unclaimed bastard mewling in a cot behind the bar at the Low Tide Arms, so let's take ourselves to The Sodden Sailor. I can quench my ache there without fear."

With this he trotted off and I hurried after him, almost stepping on his heels in my keenness not to be left behind.

Until I caught my first glimpse of the sea.

It was moving, grey and white, in the moment between two buildings across the street from me.

It was alive and stole my breath and was unlike anything I had ever seen.

Then it was gone and the dirt and the noise and the drunken men took over again.

The man who was now working for me – or so I believed – was getting away because my attention had been pulled away for a second, so I started to run, and would have run into him had the sea not returned.

We turned a corner – and there it was.

I grinned.

Amazed.

Ran forwards to the edge of the world.

Even the shrieking storm of great wild white birds circling overhead and splattering fat white drops dangerously close to where I stood did not scare me.

The sea was my new favourite thing.

The waves crashed and churned, throwing up spray that just missed my feet. They were restless and rolling and magnificent.

And there, sitting like a king on a throne of rock out in the middle of this spectacle was my dad.

My heart soared.

He was scruffy, sodden, wonderful.

I yelled out and began to run towards him. The water was over the top of my socks when I felt something sharp.

A tug.

Suddenly, I was travelling backwards, being dragged by my collar, I realised.

I whirled round. It was the man who I had paid to help me.

Not hinder.

"Let go!" I told him.

He shook his head and kept taking me away from the sea and my dad.

Eventually he set me down on lump of stone built into the dock.

He looked at me.

He looked out to sea.

"Is that your dad?" he asked.

"Yes," I snapped back.

"In that case, I'm sorry."

I stopped trying to wriggle free at this. I was confused – and I noticed that I had lost a shoe in the sea.

My mum would be furious when she found out, I thought, and, at this, it all became too much for me and I burst into tears.

The man patted me on the shoulder, and out on his rock my dad began to sing.

His voice was deep, a rumble like a storm in the distance.

The tune it carried towards us was not one I recognised. It was not one of the hymns sung every Sunday morning in Chapel by the congregation as the Minister looked down on us. It was not one of drunken laments that sometimes woke me in the night by men stumbling past outside.

It was a tune rich in melody and now his voice was soaring.

Rising above the day and leaving all in its shade.

I sat and listened and by my side the man stood gazing at his feet. He looked sad. I had no idea why.

There was someone else there as well.

A new stranger.

He was walking past me and on, into the sea. It splashed around his ankles, teased its way up to his knees as he moved deeper in.

No one grabbed him and pulled him back to shore.

Not as they had with me.

He kept walking until he was no longer walking but paddling clumsily. His head kept disappearing underwater, then broke back through.

Slowly, chaotically, he moved out to sea and long minutes later he reached the rock where my dad sat singing his strange and beautiful song.

I sat and watched, not knowing what else I could do, as the man pulled himself up onto the rock.

My dad embraced him.

Wrapped skinny, sodden arms around him.

Then dragged him back, off the rock, and into the water.

They were gone.

Alarmed by this, scared and lost, I got to my feet, turned to the man.

The creases in his face grew gentle.

"Your dad has changed," he said. "He's become a creature of the sea. A siren. There's plenty more of them. Some are beautiful and young, with hair that flows wilder than any tide, and they tempt out the rich merchant men and bloated sailors with their songs, take them under and strip their flesh clean off with their teeth and crunch their bones.

"Your dad's fare is coarser stuff, the wastrels and the drunks that he can call from here on these dirty, old docks. He sings a song for us. A song for the dregs."

He rested his hand back on my shoulder and looked in my eyes and I knew in my belly that he meant well.

"And as for you, young master," he went on, "Your dad's lost to you now, and you need to go home. I truly wish it was not the case, but it is, and there's no tears or rage or coins that can change the course of things."

Saying this, he produced the money I had given him and pressed it into my hand. Then he walked away.

Sober until he was drunk again and wise.

For my part, I did not go home. I stayed at the docks and got a job gutting fish. Now and then I found a small bone inside the gore and wondered if they had sucked it up off the

seabed, where it had fallen to rest after my dad had eaten up one more jaded jack tar.

After my shift, I would sit and watch out for him on his rock. I saw him less and less as the years passed. And when I did catch a glimpse of him, he seemed shifted, changed and more like a scrawny, slippery fish that a man.

His song grew quieter too, until I was no longer sure if it was my dad I could hear or the ocean sighing, sighing, sighing slow as the tide fell away.

Brian Maycock *lives in Glasgow and is currently writing a novel.*

Reshaping Tentacles
Jennifer Jeanne McArdle

The ocean sparkles blue and green and the waves come slow and short beyond the huge bay windows. She scares me because she calls me so strongly. If I went for a swim, I'd come undone. Can't have that. Maybe my doctor would tell me it'd be good for my health. *Unlikely*. They never suggest we lose our forms.

I'm at one of Nadia's houses. She's a famous actress that I met when I was working as a personal stylist. I'm not a stylist anymore because I kept missing appointments, but people still like having me around because I'm attractive (they call me an "ice queen"), an interesting anomaly, and I'm laid back enough to listen to their rich people bullshit without being a threat.

My skin prickles, almost loses its "proper" color, and suddenly I *have* to turn around. There's a man, in his 40s, near the light blue couch, sipping scotch and looking at me out of the corner of his eye. He smiles perfect teeth and walks towards me.

"Didn't expect to see someone like you here," he says.

"Same," I answer, trying to keep calm but my body is filling with energy. Now that he's close, all my senses feel heightened. I've experienced something like this before. But never this strongly. I know exactly what he is. I swallow my prosecco; the liquid bubbles the whole way down my throat tube.

"I'm Alex. Alexander Kallis." He offers me a hand and raises an eyebrow. He must feel it too, maybe even more so because he's older and male. Not like I know much about how our bodies work. He is playing a dangerous game, talking to me without being on suppressors. I can't resist a chance to touch him. We shake hands for longer than necessary. I feel hot and snap my hand back.

"People like us need to stick together. We should hang out sometime. You look lonely."

"It's fine. I have a twin brother."

My adopted parents call my brother, Zack, and me, Kira, twins, but we had other siblings who died before we were born. Zack is the gifted one: he immediately went into a PhD program after graduation, and now he's a rising star in underwater archaeology. I have a Bachelor's degree in business that took me seven years to complete.

"Just him? No one else like you in your life?"

"None of your business." Part of me wants to spill my entire life story, and then some, all over him.

"I'm only trying to entertain you. Why go to a party if you just want to stare quietly?" He shrugs. "It's exhausting trying to make the people around us happy while ignoring our instincts, isn't it?" He looks out the window and sighs. I can smell his breath–musky but sweet, a bit coppery and salty. I think of standing on a dock at dawn, a storm and great clouds brewing in the distance.

He continues: "That's not our ocean, but it's the closest we'll ever get to our home. You wish you could jump in. But instead, you'll keep pretending. But you have that connection to me. You know, deep down, we're *better* than them."

Alex moves closer. "You probably grew up hearing that you must be careful of someone like me, who doesn't play by the rules. But *they* aren't like us. How could they understand?" He brushes a crumb from my cheek. I fight the urge to lean my cheek into his hand, but I'm disgusted by this desire. He's not my type, visually, but I can't–

"Kira, you've met Alex," comes Shana's voice. Shana writes scripts for bad Rom-Coms on streaming services to pay the bills. I've never watched any of her stuff even though I meet her monthly for girls' brunches. "I figured you two would have things in common." She purses her lips, reminding me of a fish. Does she find this amusing? But she knows what would happen if--

"Alex is the CEO of Kallis Shipping. They've revolutionized the business of shipping bulk materials internationally," David, another friend, interjects, his voice mock deep as though he's in a commercial.

"That's wonderful for you," I say and force myself to look away from his face, which is twitching ever-so-slightly. He's struggling to keep himself together. That's a relief. "But, I was just about to leave as I have dinner plans with my parents." I smile and turn from the group.

"Wait!" Alex's voice. He stutters, and I almost feel bad for him, knowing what he must be feeling. The ache in my genitalia that started the moment I saw him grows stronger.

"Yes?" I turn. I want to embrace him. *I can't.*

"Please take my card?"

I snatch it from him without thinking.

"Ooo," says both David and Shana. I curse them silently. This isn't a game.

Late that night, I can't sleep. I never sleep well anymore because my dreams are anxious; I keep feeling like I've forgotten to do something. Am I supposed to sleep like "normal" people? Zach never has trouble sleeping, so I guess it's a *me* problem. Sometimes, I wish I had more friends like me and Zach, but I've always wanted to be normal.

I look at Alex's business card; the words and numbers separate and swim in circles. I think of being broken apart like foam in the waves, like beautifully tragic mermaids after death. I wish the normals loved us like they love mermaids. Maybe it's the long, flowing hair that attracts them. Impossible for me without a wig.

Alex would understand, wouldn't he? Not many people like us have been as successful as him in business, getting the normals to trust him. He must have good advice. I punch his number into my phone. It rings and rings, and I almost hang up, but then:

"Hello?"

I shiver. We talk for a few hours.

"Sweet dreams, Beautiful," he whispers before I hang up the phone. The sad thing is, I know he means it. I'm more beautiful to him than I've been to any man I've ever dated.

During the week, we meet up for coffee. I choose a cheap, always crowded place. He hesitates as he prefers classier places, but I insist. It's more distracting to have people around me. If we were somewhere more private, I'd be in his arms so quickly, I'd let him move his hands under my shirt, and then--

"How much brain power do we waste holding our human forms? If we didn't have to, we'd be so much smarter than them," he says. "They should be more afraid of us."

I meet with my therapist, but I'm not sure she's helpful. She advertised that she had clients like me before, with my unique biology, but she often doesn't understand my feelings. I don't mention Alex.

"Everyone who's depressed thinks they're uniquely broken. That's not special to you guys," Nadia reminds me when I call her. She's back in California. The time difference between there and here in Florida means that she's awake very early to talk to me. At least I have one good friend, even if she's not like me. I sip an ice coffee. The coldness on my fingertips has caused them to loosen. I look around, noticing tourists with fanny packs and sunburns and ugly sunglasses looking in my direction. I will my fingers back into the right shape because I can't stand when strangers know what I am. People from colder climates, who've usually never met someone like me before, ask so many intrusive questions.

How much longer can I live like this? It's painful, putting my fingers back together.

I use the good hand to text Alex.

I agree to dinner with Alex at a candlelit spot. We talk for hours. He wants me to go back to his place, but this morning, I told Zach to call me at 9PM and insist I come home. I didn't tell Zach why.

I return to my apartment, the blood rushing in my ears, my hands feeling damp, and the frustration causing my whole body to tingle. I open my door to see Zach sitting on my couch.

A warm breeze moves my pink curtains, causes my doodads hanging outside to chime. A little dog barks in the distance.

"What have you been doing?" he asks me as he rubs his left ankle.

"I was out with a friend."

"You were out with Alexander Kallis. I know his reputation. How long have you been seeing him?"

"It's only been a couple of dates, Zach." I throw myself onto the chair, pretending to be nonchalant, though I can still smell Alex. "I just wanted to connect to another Octomen. I could learn a lot from him. Real humans really respect him—"

"Kira. That's bullshit. You know what he wants from you. You're too young." A couple of tears leak from Zach's eyes. "I'm glad you finally want to connect to other Octomen, but ask me, and I'd introduce you to someone decent." I want to believe his tears, but I know it takes real effort to squeeze our muscles to release water. He knows I want to be human, so he's pretending to appeal to me.

"Zach, I'm not leaving you anytime soon."

"I know you're unhappy, Kira, but, if have sex with him, he'll impregnate you. You'll lay eggs. And you'll die."

"Yes." I sit up and roll my eyes. "I'm aware of how Octomen reproduction works. I can control myself."

"Kira, you can barely stop yourself from eating two slices of cake."

"Don't patronize me. I'm not a child." I shout louder than expected.

He sits forward. "It's not about you. Alex, unlike me, is a fertile male. The Octomen community has blacklisted him because he refuses to take hormone suppressors; he thinks they make him stupid. If he's off his suppressors and already focused on you, he won't be able to control his impulses. He'll follow you to the end of the earth if he has to. Maybe we should go to the police."

"Please, the police will just laugh. They, police, humans, don't care about what happens to Octomen. They act all self-righteous for allowing our species to live on their planet, but they fear what would happen if there were too many of us. You ever wonder what's the point of living here, when we'll never be good enough for them?"

I feel guilty, suddenly thinking of my adoptive mother. She does try. Many of them try.

But--

Zach looks out the window. "If you and Alex mate, there'll be even more of us. If existing is *so horrible* for you, then why impose it on more Octomen?"

I've never heard my cheerful brother get that dark. I've been cynical since puberty. The training I'd gone through as a child to get my many tentacles to mimic and constantly hold a human form was breaking down. My parents gave me pills. I couldn't eat. I went to the hospital for weekly injections.

One time, in gym class, I lost control when someone kicked a ball to me and my whole stomach just fell out. The tentacles forced into the shape of a human abdomen started waving free. I had to curl up so small. I couldn't scream because my faux voice box was moving inside my throat. The teachers surrounded me.

"Kira, get it together," they chanted. They thought they were helping. But I kept thinking, why is my real body so awful that I have to hide it before the other kids see it?

"It's hard, Zach," I admit. "I can't stop thinking about him and what it would be like to feel that kind of pleasure...and relief."

He shakes his head. "I'm invited to the annual International Academic Conference for Octomen Research. You should join me. All the fertile male Octomen attending have to be on hormone suppressors. I know you haven't wanted to go before, but it might be good for you. Maybe your attraction to Alex isn't just physical–you're finally realizing that you need Octomen friends."

I never liked having Octomen friends before because I thought we were *trying* to be human. What if I spend too much time with Octomen and lose control and revert back to Octomen habits? But perhaps Zach was right. He seemed happier than me. He studies our species' past, riding in submarines down to our crashed spaceships that escaped from a dying planet hundreds of years ago. His Octomen body didn't need air to breathe, and he could work in the extreme pressure. He must be so much stronger than me to hold his human form, even in the ocean.

Like most Octomen, my birth parents waited until near the end of their lives to reproduce. My mother died shortly after. After we hatched from eggs nourished in an artificial womb, our Octomen father and the researchers at the

Octomen Reproduction Institute trained us on how to take human shapes, speak, eat, and live like humans. Although Octomen naturally mimic other creatures, we need years of training to perfect a human shape so accurately that most people can't tell we aren't human.

Our father died when we were five-years-old, and we were adopted by an infertile male Octomen and his human partner. My brother is also an infertile male.

"It's obvious why so many of our eggs fail and why so many of us have health problems. How much better off would our species be if we weren't pumping our males full of suppressors and our females weren't decrepit by the time they lay eggs? If we were healthy, we'd rule this planet." Alex had told me.

When Octomen first arrived on Earth, our ancestors made a deal with humans. We could live on Earth, but as fake humans. Our true forms, which were similar to Earth's octopuses, but with thousands of small tentacles on our skin, covering our bodies and eight large tentacles, were frightening to them.

Octomen is what they called us. I don't even know what language my ancestors spoke, what we called ourselves, what holidays we celebrated, or anything about our home planet, except that it had a vast ocean.

I get an email from Alex after I stop talking to him for a week:

"Why are you so worried about death? You'll be free of your pain. I will bring you true joy. Don't deny your nature. Maybe you're unhappy because you aren't meant to live this long."

There is no AC used during the Octomen Conference. For once, the atmosphere is for us, not for humans. The windows are wide open, letting in the hot humidity. One panel discusses how to manage the pain we get from forcing our tentacles into alien shapes. I meet Octomen chefs. They encourage us to put food directly into our true mouths, which are hiding in our chests. I become pleasantly full on chewy creatures from the ocean floor.

At night, I see a dance by Octomen who expertly reshape their bodies, stretch and wiggle their tentacles along with the beats of instruments unplayable by human hands but magical and complex in Octomen tentacles. Everyone is happier and freer here, but they are nervous about any human reporters or outside media.

"Octomen are getting more brazen," I tell Zach. "When we were kids, they would have been afraid to ever lose their human shapes, even among other Octomen."

"It's been generations now that we've been here. The good humans know we aren't here to hurt them. Many humans finally understand that if they let us be ourselves, we might be able to help them, too. Like, if I was allowed to work on human shipwrecks, I could bring them so much knowledge about their history. You would have seen some of this change, if you spent more time with Octomen and weren't wasting your time being a novel toy for your rich 'friends'"

I've been a poor sister, and he resents me. I wish I could loosen my tentacles, too, but fear grips me. *We can never not be human.* That's what my family and my teachers told me. But, I am able to sleep well for a couple of nights.

Alex sends flowers to my house. It's a bouquet of odd blooms with strong smells, like deep red pitcher plants, delicate sundew, skinny yellow-eyed glass, and sour cranberries. The smell reminds me of him. I spend most of the night reading everything I can about Alexander Kallis on the internet.

Innovator. Businessman. Charismatic.

Exploitative. Abusive. Reviews of employees complain about the lack of benefits, the long shifts, and the unpunished harassment from their superiors. He threatens to sue everyone. He pushes smaller contractors around. He busts up unions and buys up small trucking businesses. He wants to swallow the world.

Rumor said he's fathered several Octomen children. But he paid people off, stalled DNA tests, and skated responsibility.

I remember to close all my tabs, but I fall asleep in my big chair by the computer. Zach wakes me up a few hours later.

"Kira, you can't miss the last day of the conference."

I wander the halls of the building, watching the little lizards crawl along the walls, feeling like I'm floating out of myself. I wish I could make myself wish I'd never met Alex. Zach is busy schmoozing with potential donors for his research, which I won't interrupt. I find an open room and look at the conference topic:

"Octomen Reproduction: What are we missing?"

My therapist would tell me to avoid such a triggering topic in the woozy state that I'm in, but I shuffle inside and find a chair. The person talking is human, which turns me off a bit. I'm starting to enjoy the camaraderie of my fellow species.

"So many Octomen eggs don't survive in the artificial 'wombs'. How did the Octomen reproduce before they had technology to create artificial wombs? The female is responsible for laying the eggs, but fertile males, sort of like Earth's own seahorses, also have a role in reproduction beyond just providing sperm. Our research, albeit controversial, provides clear answers."

I am enraptured by slides describing Octomen biology in greater detail than I've ever seen before. My head is buzzing with possibilities.

Alex is out of town for a few weeks, but finally, we are able to meet again. He takes me on his yacht to his house in the Keys. He plays soft, romantic music and feeds me a steak dinner. I miss the music and food from the conference. Still, I am human enough that this is somewhat romantic. Funny, he keeps advising me to embrace my instinct, but outside of wanting to mate with me and a few small gestures, he works pretty hard to seem human.

We hold hands as the sun goes down while we sit by his pool. He tries kissing me, but instead we both fall out of shape. Wrapping each other in our tentacles, I struggle to get to the water because I'm not used to moving in my natural state. He expertly pulls me towards the pool. How many times has he done this before?

We swirl around each other, total pleasure fills me from my tentacle tips to my brain in my center. I close my eyes, falling into a rainbow of colors, tingling vibrations. Stress seeps out of each of my strained muscles. When his organs pierce me, the pain is unbearable but also dizzying, euphoric.

After the act is finished, I float for several moments, pure bliss. When the feeling starts to wane, I pull myself out of the pool. It takes nearly twenty minutes for me to put myself back into human shape.

"There's a boat waiting for you near the dock," Alex tells me coolly after I get dressed. "We'll talk again before you're ready to lay the eggs. Gail, my assistant, will get them to a facility with an artificial womb."

Predictably, Alex does not call me over the next few days. The time for me to lay is coming soon. I've been talking to an Octomen friend I met at the conference. She's a dancer, an expert at changing her shape.

When I first met Alex's assistant, Gail, Alex joked that I looked enough like her that we could be sisters. My dancer friend coaches me on how to change the shape of my tentacles, so I can look exactly like her. I have a wig that matches her hair.

I go to Alex's office after normal hours at around 6:30PM. At the main entrance, another employee recognizes "Gail" and holds a glass door open for me, so I can enter.

"I forgot my cell phone upstairs," I tell the security guard.

"No big deal. Alex is still in his office, I think."

I take the elevator up to Alex's office, walking past the real Gail's desk. I knock on Alex's door.

Alex sees me through the window of his office. He gets up to open the door. Before he can smell that it's actually me, I shove my right hand forcefully into his side, piercing through his tentacles and grabbing the hidden sack.

He moans in pleasure and pain as I pull the sack out from his tentacles and towards me. I push my own organ out from my thigh, up from under my skirt. When the two organs meet, he falls out of his human shape, his clothes ripping apart, buttons ricocheting around the room, and then he stops moving.

I pump my eggs into his womb. His tentacles are drawn close to his center and they harden, their color going from pale blue to dark green.

The Octomen reproduction lecturer explained this would happen at the conference:

"After the female deposits her eggs into the male's womb, he immediately becomes an immobile, protective shell."

Now, I am exhausted, but female Octomen survive several hours after laying eggs, and usually exhibit a last burst of impressive strength. I drag Alex's body down the back stairs, out the emergency exit, and to my car. I drive back home, text my brother to come to my house, and leave a letter for him.

> *"Forgive me, Zach. I wish I was like you, and could accept myself. But I feel like a monster. I've been trying forever to be happy, but nothing has worked. I lied when I said I could resist Alex. He's been all I can think about and resisting him only adds to my torture. But I love you and the idea that a little girl like me might grow up with the chance to love herself, in a better society you and the others hope to build. Please, take care of my children—Alex won't be able to hurt anyone else again, either. Our species deserves a chance to be beautiful and happy again."*

> *"We theorize that infertile males are a natural third sex for Octomen. They are meant to take on the parent role, raising their sisters' children."*

My house is not far from the shore. I drag my wobbly legs to my car and get in, catching my reflection in the mirror. Holes from where bits of my tentacles have fallen off dot my face and my coloring has faded to a slimy gray. I arrive at the beach, get out, drag my feet, and then crawl to the end of the dock.

The waves pull me as if I'm the tide herself at the mercy of moon gravity. I fall completely apart and push myself forward, a *plop* as I hit the water.

Not as graceful as a mermaid, but I'll become sea-foam, just the same.

> *"As the eggs grow, the father's body provides nutrition and protection. After they hatch, Octomen newborns eat their way out of their father's corpse."*

Jennifer Jeanne McArdle

Jennifer works in conservation and lives in New York. More info on her website: www./jenniferjeannemcardle.blogspot.com/

Food Chain

Morgan Melhuish

At low tide they converge, winkle pickers and oyster catchers - not the birds, though they are there too, turnstones and sanderlings, starlings even, picking through the sun dried weed - but men, hunting.

Alan used to come down here with his dad and so the lad knows some of the older gents. He nods to them politely but keeps walking along the edge of the bay, past their rusting bikes. He watches their forms become silhouettes in the sun, as they wade out, through silt and mud, carrying spades and towing blue plastic crates for their spoils.

If there's a good haul all the public houses will announce *Mussels & Fresh Seafood Available* tomorrow lunchtime. Alan wouldn't touch it with a barge pole, the filth that's dumped around here, and that's before the microplastics and flame retardants they've now found in fish.

It shouldn't go back into the food chain. Everyone knows that. But it does.

The men treat the shore like his mum frequents charity shops, eagle-eyed, talons sharp as her polished nails finger geegaws and bric-à-brac, sifting for gems.

There are dredgers and crabbers, lug worm hunters seeking bait, the odd detectorist brandishing a swish bit of kit, wired for sound and listening for the tell tale submarine pings of metal.

Alan ignores them, the dog walkers and joggers, courting couples huddled into one another, spooning down by the breakwater rocks. He pushes on, past them all, seeking a little peace.

It's gone 8pm and yet the sun has at least an hour's reign before it sets.

Glints of summer light are caught in trickles and pools, reflected in what's left of the retreating tide.

It's in one of these pools that Alan sees it, shimmering with a coat of black mud. It's like a basking seal or the hull of a row boat, the dark bloated shape mirrored in the brine. He stares at it, shields his eyes to try and make out exactly what it is.

Once, he and his father had found a bag full of pups, drowned runts, their young bodies all angular bones, slick with estuary slime despite their sack cloth covering. It was like peeling away the layers of time, reaching back to the primordial world and unearthing some, as yet, undiscovered creature. The boy had egged his father on, excited by the prospect of treasure, until young Alan realised they were dead dogs and he retched and splattered the claggy foreshore with his undigested dinner.

He pushes the memory down, but he can't deny that his first thought was that this shape is a body. It wouldn't be the first time one has washed up, an upturned paddleboarder swept away, a swimmer caught out of their depth, a desperate migrant hoping for a better life.

With all the grace of gangly adolescence Alan clambers off the path and over the large boulders that line the bay, supposedly a defence against winter gales and tides.

His boots crunch against stones and then a scattering of slippery weed coated pebbles decreasing in size the closer he gets to the water line.

He slides towards the object, arms out like a surfer to aid his balance. Amongst the dark silt tangles of vibrant green sea lettuce add a shot of colour, the dirty mustard of kelp hisses and pops under his feet. More than once Alan lifts his boot free from a tangle of seaweed strands like the cord of his headphones. His life feels significant, more cinematic with a constant soundtrack. Especially now, close to this discovery.

It reminds Alan of a mermaid's purse laying on the silt, the tough embryonic membrane coddling a baby dog fish or skate. Only this is huge, the amniotic sac of a calf, it seems to wobble faintly, to throb with bloated life. It looks to Alan as if it might burst at any moment, and something emerge.

Alan reaches for his mobile to take a picture. His fingers slide across the screen as tentacles, dark as squid ink spaghetti, seep around his slowly sinking feet.

It came from us. The things we let flow back into the water.

Born in a primordial soup of shit and piss, oestrogen and crude oil, spawned from sarin and the remnants of dumped biological warfare.

It spread, this wonderful new thing, amorphous as the sea itself. Fused by dancing lightning in a summer storm, coalescing into something living.

It emerged, over time, a hybrid of kelp and the polymer chains of tossed plastic partially degraded.

It recognised the calm of this place, coming to the bay to give birth.

The organism sensed Alan was there, felt his tread, the quivering vibrations of his tinny music, the pulse of blood quickening with his wonder.

With each of Alan's steps, into the mucky web, it has tracked its prey. It needs sustenance.

Now it tightens its grip.

Alan topples, a felled trunk.

The glare of the sun is in his eyes. He squints in his descent, feels the air punched from his lungs as the ground is harder than silt and muddy rock has any right to be. He feels the tug at his ankles, twists and tries to find purchase in the ooze.

Within moments he is filth itself, a bog creature, a tar baby.

Alan kicks out instinctively, his body scrabbles against his unseen assailant. He groans and pants understanding the need to fight, to do anything to survive.

His vision, flecked with grime, tells his mind unbelievable things, that he is being dragged under the sludge of low tide by seaweed fronds. He'd think it crazy if it wasn't happening so quickly.

Desperately, Alan reaches out and seizes the blubbery mass he came to investigate. His nails dig deep trying to find an anchor, clawing at the gelatinous womb.

For a moment there is respite, Alan feels the squeeze around his ankles slacken. He increases the pressure.

This sensation is new. Suffering.

It has felt its prey struggle and strain before, the writhing of scales and fins, the beat of wings against the water. It has felt terror but only vicariously. Now it shudders in pain receptors it didn't know it had.

The wean is at risk.

It is coming.

A cat's cradle of tentacles rise up, thin whips thrash at the air, slap the muddy ground all around Alan. Some find their mark and he cries out at the lashing. He balls up, foetal in the silt.

Alan takes a moment, breathes in peaty, briny muck, tries to ignore the lacerations raining down on him. Fight turns to thoughts of flight. He scrabbles in the dirt to get upright and he half stumbles, half skids and rolls away.

The tentacles do not pursue him, instead they wriggle and pulsate. Alan watches as the mermaid's purse bursts, a flood of viscous white, molten plastic drenching the dark mire.

Within the remains of the sac the wean shifts. It is fish nor fowl, recasting itself in the mould of memories, adapting and altering its form. It is fin and beak and frond, claw and gill, blade, bladder and holdfast. It is a sticky multitude, mesmerising Alan in its possibility. He has just the one form, dirtied and hurting, incredulous in the slime.

The jellied wean flops like a fish, elongates, grows limbs.

It is bipedal now but still a half-formed thing.

"What are you?" The lad wonders aloud.

The stump of the creature's head slowly turns Alan's way and the teen feels he's made an awful mistake.

In the time it takes him to gasp, the creature is a plasticky golem mimicking his shape. Features form, in a stifled yawning pliant stretch; a mouth cavity, eyes blinking gloopy remnants away, two stubby ears. It is a mannequin, naked in its birth, aping him.

Strands of the viscous liquid drip down its chin as it tries to form the words Alan said.

"Waa aaaar ooo."

"I'm Alan. I'm human," the boy tells the thing, growing in confidence.

"Eye Al an. Oo man." It is a quick study.

The synthetic doppelgänger takes a step towards him, its foot squelching in the mud. It finds its balance, Alan recognises the surfing gesture he made not long ago.

In the sunset the figure looks like one of those Anthony Gormley statues they studied at school. It is art, this changeling.

Alan gazes as its surface refines, a true mirror image. It stands face to face, toe to toe, its breath mingling with his.

For a strange second Alan thinks the reflection will kiss him.

Alan forgets to be scared as it reaches out.

There are two boys embracing, stood in silt.

The creature finds the weakest point in itself, in its adversary, and quickly snaps the lad's neck without hesitation.

A rush of tentacles flow through the sea's sediment to feed on the discarded child. There is something about the still warm flesh that makes it long for more.

Still evolving, 'Alan' strides to the shore. With anticipation he looks forward to his continued metamorphosis, his final state.

The evening breeze is chill on his skin and Alan can taste industry on the air. He breathes in carbon and sulphur, fills his lungs with fossil fuels and greenhouse gasses. To him they are sweet.

He is used to the polluted water but this is all new. He has no words for what he sees, but it doesn't stop him appreciating the rotting spears of a long gone pier, green fields of potatoes inland, the jaundiced yellow rape nearly ready for harvest.

Alan climbs the breakwater rocks, gaining a view over the whole bay. There are others like him, in the mud, dragging crates of dirty clams onto the shore. Alan licks his lips at the thought of these cocklepickers. They will make choice flesh for the weans to come.

He watches as one of the scavengers drinks thirstily, discarding the empty bottle in one toss before wiping his wet mouth. Another produces a brand new packet of cigarettes, the cellophane wrapper shines as it flutters away, caught on the wind. The old man curses but doesn't stoop to pick it up.

Alan sits on a rock, smelling the burning tar and nicotine, watching the sunset. He's mesmerised by the streaks of scarlet and lilac, the dazzling orange globe slowly disappearing on the horizon. It's a beautiful world he's been born into.

When the tide flows in the things the men have discarded will be carried away. Other pods will surface, floating chains of polymers, his brethren, ready to hatch and break free. A new life cycle will begin, a new food chain.

Alan will welcome them.

Morgan Melhuish *has work published or accepted by Bag of Bones Press, Ghost Orchid Press and Timber Ghost Press.*

Friends of the Sea Witch
Helena O'Connor

The nights out of water pass in a blur. I emerge only to feed on lost souls. It's easy to find those who won't be missed, society's outcasts. Those I suck dry sate my hunger, but there's an emptiness growing inside me. What is it all for? How long since I felt alive?

I pick up a random guy online and we meet at a bar. A place with cocktails named after poets, and trendy tables stained blood red. Fish swimming in the walls. I like the sound of bubbling water; it feels like home.

"Hard work to keep the tanks clean." The guy looks at the fish, wide eyed. His chin dimples when he smiles. His name is Raymond. Or Rory. Something with an R. These human names all sound the same.

"They belong in the sea." A clown fish dodges through the tentacles of a fake anemone. Does it notice the anemone doesn't sting? Can a tame fish know something it's never felt? Does a remnant of electric contact still live within its genes? I wonder if it misses the sharp reminders of being alive that permeate life in the sea. I know I do. But food in the ocean is scarce these days. Any creature that can feed on land must if it wants to survive.

"You must be fun at parties." Rodger, or Redmond, is mocking me.

I rearrange my features into an alluring smile. "Oh, but I am. So much fun." A seductive wink and he's hooked, line and sinker. Those qualities they champion; sense of humor, shared interests, all that human ephemera… it matters little once the scent of sex muddies the waters.

He follows me home like a lost dog. "You live here?" The tone isn't judgmental, just filled with wonder. My house reflects me—a bedazzling sea witch cavern made of glimmering mermaid colors. It's very shiny, my lair, all part of my captivating essence. My victims are so busy looking for pearls, they never notice the jaws of the giant clamshell closing around them.

"Not what I was expecting, but I love it." His face is an open book. The honesty is refreshing, vulnerable. Once victims enter the lair, most adopt a bravado they think will win favor and quickly lead to the bedroom. As if stepping into my home was not enough to seal the deal. But not Rebus…. Roland? He seems genuinely interested in me, as a person. I've not encountered this before.

"Any pets?"

"No." When I answer too quickly, he seems taken aback.

"Not a fan? I love animals. I volunteer at this pet shelter across town…" His voice drones into the background as I prepare to feast. The juices gestate in my abdomen, ready to dissolve his bones. Ryan… Riley… Rowan? has already been here longer than most. The way he's wandering around, inspecting my shelves… it's impudent. I should be offended, but the curiosity in his deep brown eyes, the innocence, makes him seem like a lost little fish, searching for the sting of the tentacles it depends upon. "You really live in this great big house, all alone?

"Of course." To be honest, I spend most days in the sea, but I can hardly say that. I've amassed a wealth of ship-wreck treasure to build this lair. A witch needs a certain kind of place to lure her prey. We have our standards. My sense of pride bristles at his tone. "Don't you like it?"

He takes another look around. "No, I do. I really do. This place is amazing, it just… seems a little lonely." He pulls me to the sofa where we curl up together. He doesn't seem to care whether we have sex or not (spoiler alert, we do), he seems happy just to be here. The company is quite nice. As I relax in his embrace, the emptiness recedes momentarily. In an impulse decision, I don't kill him.

I tell myself it's an experiment. The thrill of the kill will be greater if I get to know this human. Once I've earned his trust, betrayal will sweeten his flesh. I fall into a pattern with Robert (I learned his actual name, don't read into it). I suppose some would call this pattern 'dating.' Not me, obviously, but a human might.

One day he brings me a kitten. The thing is so scrawny it can barely stand. Its fur is black as the cavernous night. "What's this for?" I eye the furry intruder with apprehension. As a rule, sea creatures do not like cats.

"I know you're not an animal person, but this little one lost her mother, they strayed onto the highway looking for food…" His voice tells the full story, as do the tears tracking down his cheeks. Robert is such an emotional creature, and he really loves animals. I eyeball the kitten where it mewls on the floor. I suppose we have something in common, this stray and me. Robert must have remembered that I have no parents.

"What does it eat?"

He hands me a bag of supplies. "I'll leave you two to get acquainted." He looks over his shoulder, eyes crinkling in a beneficent smile. "Just give it some time, I know you two will hit it off."

I call her Mina, Princess of the Ravening Depths. It does take time to get used to the warmth of another presence. The first time Mina claws her way onto my bed and snuggles against me, licking my hand, I recoil in horror. But as the nights pass, I seek her out her fur and warmth.

When Robert next visits, Mina is curled on my shoulder being conveyed about the house, purring all the while. Robert's dimples light up his whole face. "I knew you'd love her!"

"I do." Mina has been a revelation. I never countenanced the idea it might be nice to share a life with someone. I smile at Robert, where he reclines on the sofa. I was right not to kill him the night we met. This is so much more satisfying.

The next night, a cold rain blows in from the east with the icy tendrils of a sea witch wind. Mina ruffles her fur and snuggles into her new bed. I have discovered online shopping and Mina now has her own mini sea cave, bedecked with every bedazzling cat thing I can find. I spoil her.

"I'm making soup, little girl. A nice hot soup to warm us from the winds." I stir my cauldron while Mina purrs contentment, yellow eyes shining. It's so much more meaningful, making soup for someone else, instead of always eating alone. I hope Robert knows how much he has brought to my life, with this revelation of companionship. The warmth of company spreads through me almost as heartily as the aroma from my pot. This soup is the best I've ever made. Tonight, we shall surely feast.

I pull a femur from the pot and suck it dry. I was right to wait. Robert's bones are so much sweeter, because of his trust. Mina mews, awaiting her share. This is the first soup we've brewed together, and it will hardly be the last. There's plenty more Roberts in the dating pool, plenty more fish in the sea.

The nights out of water pass in the happiness of company. Two sea-witches in their lair. I have finally found meaning in my life, the emptiness is gone. There is such wonderful, simple joy in sharing someone, devouring the meat from their bones, together with the someone I love.

Helena O'Connor is an Australian writer with short fiction published in Aurealis, Andromeda Spaceways Magazine and Nature: Futures.

Isadora's Trunk
K.G. Anderson

"Turning to piracy, are we, Captain?" Huw Jones, slight but wiry, frowned at the old-fashioned slat trunk that took up the better part of my cabin. "That trunk looks like it should be filled with gold doubloons."

"Don't I wish!" I handed my first officer a tumbler of Old Forester. "That way, there'd be some money in the proposition."

He gave a short, dry laugh. Then we clinked glasses in a toast to the voyage—a first-night tradition since Jones had joined my crew at the end of the Great War. Despite that peculiar squall that had hit just as we'd left Southampton, the *Atlantis Quest* was making good speed towards the Mediterranean.

I sipped, then regarded the battered black trunk. "That trunk is here as a favor to an old...friend. She wants me to drop it overboard as we pass Gibraltar."

Jones raised a sandy eyebrow. "How very odd. Well, if it's not doubloons, what in God's name is in the thing?"

"Just some papers. Or so I'm told." I picked up the bottle. "A little more?"

"My career is over," Isadora Beeswit had written on heavily perfumed and elaborately monogrammed stationery. "I'm haunted by despair."

Oh, good God. I dimly recalled that my erstwhile fiancée did something or other in New York publishing and I certainly wished her well with it. Primarily because it pretty much ensured that our paths would never cross again. Our brief romance, some 20 years earlier, had reached a stormy conclusion when she'd got herself engaged to two--no, I think it was three--other fellows. One of them quite a dicey character.

"These things happen, Leland," she'd said airily--as if that were an explanation. Well, these things certainly did not happen to Leland Clayburn, and I'd cut her off decisively. If I'd had regrets, those were long forgotten. Anyway, that frou-fra was enough to put me off marriage for good. After that fling with Isadora, life on the high seas for the past 28 years had proved comfortingly humdrum.

"I've locked all my worthless manuscripts in a trunk and sent them to England, care of your shipping company," she'd written. "Leland, I want you to promise me you'll hurl the cursed thing overboard! Let it sink into the turbulent waters off Gibraltar! Surely, in view of our tragically broken engagement, you do owe me this one, small favor."

Tragically? Small? After Jones left, I reassessed how much room her damn trunk was taking up in my cabin. For crying out loud, could the woman *really* have that many manuscripts? Why hadn't she just hired some New York carter to trundle the trunk down the street and tip it into the Hudson? And why did the trunk have a manila tag on which someone had scrawled in red ink "DO NOT OPEN! EVER!"?

On our third day at sea, I came up with a practical use for Isadora's baggage. The Southampton newsstand had misplaced my orders for *Astounding* and *Weird Tales*. In search of something to read before bed, I found myself eyeing Isadora's trunk.

What on earth could her stories be like? She wrote what they called "women's fiction," the sort of thing where star-crossed romances came dramatically uncrossed in the final pages. Well, maybe it was time to broaden my literary horizons. If Isadora was writing about romances, perhaps she'd hearkened back to our long-ago entanglement. What that had lacked in sincerity it had certainly made up for in drama.

I examined the trunk. *"DO NOT OPEN"* indeed! Why, the tiny ornamental padlock Isadora had used to secure the big trunk practically *invited* picking.

I soon removed the lock, lifted the lid, and immediately wrinkled my nose. A scent of mildew rose from the leather-and-wool interior. Something chill and wispy brushed my face, and I batted it away. *Cobwebs, surely.* The manuscripts were in heavy manila envelopes. There were fewer than I'd expected, given the trunk's size and weight. I pulled out a few and read the titles penned on the flaps: *The Flame and the Feather. Her Master's Desire. The Ambassador's Heart.*

I smirked as I drew *The Ambassador's Heart* slowly, tenderly from its manila sheath--*good heavens, was her writing getting to me already?*--and settled back in my armchair. The story turned out to be a surprisingly spicy read. The insights into the protagonist's mind as she stalked her masculine prey were only slightly more horrifying than the latest Lovecraft story I'd read in *Weird Tales*. I was well into *The Ambassador's Heart* when eight bells signaled midnight. I fell into bed, turned out the lamp, and enjoyed the last peaceful night's sleep that I, or anyone else aboard the *Atlantis Quest*, would have for a fortnight.

It's my custom to eat breakfast with the men coming off the morning watch. But that morning two of the burly stokers nearly ran me down in the corridor. Their faces showed frustration, confusion, and--though I found it hard to believe--fear. One of the men held a tiny yellow chick.

"What's going on?"

"I don't rightly know, sir."

"Cheep!"

The man looked so unhappy that I let him go. In the galley, Benjamin, our cook, was anxious to provide details. He pointed to little yellow chicks, just the like one the stoker carried, bouncing around on the floor of the galley, chirping.

"The eggs hatched," he said.

"Don't eggs have to be warm to do that? And underneath chickens?"

"Yes! And I had them in the cooler!" Benjamin pointed with a spatula at the old walk-in cooler.

I yanked opened the door and checked. Plenty chilly inside, for sure. Out in the mess, men were opening the lids of serving plates. I was reassured to see that the dishes contained perfectly ordinary sausages and bacon. It would certainly have been inconvenient to have piglets trotting around the ship. "So the problem is just the eggs, then?"

"For now," Benjamin said. "We'll see about lunch."

"Well, just skip the eggs and fry more bacon. We'll figure this out."

"The morning watch had quite the breakfast," I remarked when Jones came on the bridge. "Chickens!"

"Livened things up quite a bit, Captain," he said "You get these things once in a while. When I was working the *Neptune's Crown* out of Genoa we once had a hail of fish come down out of a blue sky."

Oddly, at 1100 hours, a pile of live fish--Atlantic sole, to be precise--appeared on the deck of the *Atlantis Quest*. I ordered Benjamin to pan fry them, and they made an excellent lunch.

"Strange goings on," Jones muttered.

I shrugged. Strange things might be transpiring on the *Atlantis Quest*, but I'd dealt with strange things before. Thus far, the worst that had happened was extra bacon for breakfast and some fresh fish for lunch. But I changed my mind later that afternoon when Jones stepped onto the bridge and signaled for my attention.

"What's it now, Jones? Lambs in the laundry? Bats in the belfry? Crows in the crows' nest?"

He answered with a shrill chuckle. His smile looked painted on. "The steward says there's a problem in your quarters, sir."

"Oh, for God's sake." We strode through the cramped corridors to my cabin. Our head steward stood outside the closed door, clutching a stack of fresh towels.

"Well?" Getting no answer, I flung open the door. And gaped. It appeared that a typhoon had struck my usually ship-shape accommodations. I narrowed my eyes. On close observation, the scene indicated not mayhem, but deliberate mischief.

My clothes were strewn about the room. Starched shirts were heaped on the floor, with polished shoes set neatly on top of them. One of my caps sat perched atop a wall sconce. A chair had been overturned, and a pair of my paisley print drawers dangled rakishly from one chair leg.

I turned to Jones. "Get all hands on deck in thirty minutes."

"You think you can spot the culprit, sir?" he said.

"Hell no. But I think I can put an end to it. I'm going to offer a reward. With 50 people keeping an eye out for anything out of the ordinary, the man responsible for this mischief will either stop it or spend the rest of this voyage in the brig."

"Begging to disagree, sir."

"Really? Well, let's hear *your* plan."

"It's not a plan, Captain. It's more of a...theory." Jones licked his lips. He darted glances around the ransacked cabin.

"Yes? Yes?"

"With all due respect, Captain," Jones squared his jaw,

"I think we have a demon aboard. An imp, if you will."

Damn. Seamen are notoriously superstitious, but I'd never seen any sign of it from Jones before. I opened my desk drawer and brought out the Old Forester. The man needed a drink. I handed him a fortifying shot and poured one for myself. "Now I've been in shipping for nearly 30 years and--"

"Augh!" Jones flung his glass in the air and staggered back against the wall. "Don't," he waved his arms wildly, "drink that!"

I looked down at the glass on the desk in front of me and sniffed, first cautiously and then with disgust. *Vinegar!* "Augh!"

"We have a demon, sir," Jones insisted. He held one forefinger to his lips and with the other pointed insistently at Isadora's trunk in the corner of the cabin. Which now seemed to me to be dark and belligerent. Even taunting.

A demon? But of course! "DO NOT OPEN. EVER." With that tempting label, the devious Isadora had baited her trap. And I'd stepped right into it. Again. Not only was her demon now wreaking havoc aboard my ship, *I* was the one responsible for unleashing it.

I leaped to my feet. "The hell with Gibraltar. Get this thing over the side right now!"

"Yes, sir!" Jones opened the door and shouted, which brought two burly crewmen thundering down the corridor. Under Jones' supervision, they lifted the trunk and muscled it out of the cabin.

"And open the damned lid so the damn thing sinks," I bellowed after them. Then I headed for the bridge, where I watched the trunk as it disappeared, slowly and finally, beneath the gray-green waves. *Jones had better keep his mouth shut about demons.*

With an abundance of caution, I took up temporary quarters in one of the freighter's two passenger cabins. It was musty and cramped, and the narrow bunk left much to be desired. Around 3 a.m. I got up and reached for the unopened bottle of French brandy I'd brought along. Then I stopped, hand hovering over the bottle. If a demon could hatch chicks in a refrigerator and turn Old Forester to vinegar, it could certainly ruin a fine brandy. I found myself overcome by a strange urge to lower my head to my hands and weep. With a groan, I realized I got that idea from reading *The Ambassador's Heart*.

"I think we're free of it, sir!" Jones said. The *Atlantis Quest* had loaded on cargo in Genoa without incident, steamed south through the Straits of Messina, and was now anchored in the Sicilian port of the same name.

I had moved back into my quarters, but did not share Jones' optimism about the demon. Standing at the rail, I frowned to see glowering gray clouds gathering over the Libyan coast to the south. "Stay on alert, Jones. When the chandler brings in the new supply of eggs, put a watch on the galley, round the clock. Meanwhile, I want you personally to inspect every box of cargo that leaves this ship."

"You think the demon could be hiding in one?" Jones looked worried--probably about my sanity.

"No. But if it is, rush *that* box off the ship at full speed."

I tried not to think of the incoming weather as an omen. But, of course, it was. No sooner had we steamed out of Messina and entered the Ionian Sea than the storm came roaring up and our demon resumed its nefarious work. Three crates of Bordeaux came mysteriously unsecured, sending bottles crashing about in the hold. A man on the midnight watch reported, with much reluctance, that he'd seen a ghostly figure--in pirate garb, no less!--brandishing a sword on the slippery deck. Someone had entered my cabin and my clean laundry had been neatly refolded--

every damned piece of it inside out.

I donned storm gear and helped Jones and the crew secure the cargo on the deck. All the while I cursed Isadora Beeswit, her trunk and her--now *my*--demon.

Three days later, our storm-battered ship dropped anchor off the Greek island of Taklos. The tiny picture-book harbor of Safatia sparkled in the afternoon sun as an exhausted Jones supervised the off-loading of cargo onto a barge.

"Everything accounted for, sir," he reported. "Except, of course, the wine."

I gave a bitter chuckle. We were resupplying a joint British-German archeological expedition engaged, with the help of some wealthy tourists, in plundering the site of an ancient Ionian temple. These were the sort of folks who'd certainly notice a shortage of wine.

The crew, granted shore leave, headed straight for the local tavernas. I went ashore as well, checking in to the picturesque tourist hotel on the town square. I was sitting on the hotel veranda, punishing myself with a dubious vodka and thinking dark thoughts about my cursed ship, when a distinguished-looking gentleman approached.

"Captain Clayburn of the *Atlantis Quest*? I am Professor Jonathan Vance-Pickett."

I grunted in acknowledgment and was immediately ashamed of my rudeness. "Excuse my gruffness, Professor. It's been a difficult voyage. That storm we came through, and--well--I hope your supplies arrived in order?"

The British professor, who looked like Father Christmas prepared for a brisk, tweedy hike, gave a regretful smile. "With the unfortunate exception of my Bordeaux."

"My first mate has radioed our company. Your wine will be replaced, at our expense, and shipped to the island next month."

"Thank you." Father Christmas inclined his head. "I

understand your ship is experiencing some unusual difficulties. My research assistant talked with the local stevedores, who talked with your crew."

I was appalled. "They aren't supposed to--"

"Oh, Captain," Father Christmas shook his head. "You can't stop people talking. It seems as though your ship has an imp. A demon. In the local parlance, a *daemon*."

"Well, it certainly has a *something*." I lifted the bottle, filled a glass, and put it in front of him. "Professor, I've been in the shipping business for more than 28 years and I've never seen anything like it. But perhaps you have?"

"Yes." The professor turned and indicated a robust young man at a table near the door. "I think you'll want to talk with Niko Demetrios."

I'd taken the fellow with wild black ringlets for a local fisherman, but Vance-Pickett said he was a student from the University of Athens, now serving as a research assistant to the expedition. "Having grown up here on Taklos, Niko has been of great assistance to the expedition in dealing with local traditions and beliefs. Things work a bit differently on the island, we find." He beckoned to the young man, who hurried over.

"We are discussing the captain's *daemon*, Niko," the professor said after making introductions. "Do we understand, Captain Clayburn, that it was sent by your former wife?"

"Wife?" I recoiled, rattling the tiny café table. "I'm certainly not--oh, wait. Yes. Wife? It was an old sweetheart. Not much of a sweetheart, actually. More of a--anyway, she's a ladies fiction writer. In New York."

"A writer?" The professor raised bushy eyebrows above twinkling eyes. "Imaginative!"

"Imaginative?" I snorted. "The *Atlantis Quest* is a shambles. Two of my best crewmen jumped ship in Sicily and I can't say I blame them. We hit a storm three nights ago that nearly scuttled the ship. My first mate is an absolute trouper, but even he is wearing out under the strain." I did not mention that the demon had replaced a cherished photograph of Jones' sweetheart with a cartoon of a squid.

"There are people on the island possessing the necessary resources with which to aid you," Demetrios said. His English was nearly fluent and his accent charming.

"Can the local priest do an exorcism?" I looked over the whitewashed Orthodox church on the far side of the cobblestone square.

Vance-Pickett wrinkled his nose. "I'm certain the priest would refuse. This is a small island, Captain. There's too much of a risk that your demon might get loose here."

I sighed. "Oh yes, I get it. Nobody wants it. Of course."

Young Demetrios cleared his throat. "I know people who could, ah, capture it. For a fee. You have to transport it from the island when your ship departs, Captain, but that would be perfectly safe. As safe as it was before someone opened your trunk."

I winced. *Someone,* indeed. "But how on earth do you propose to catch this thing? None of us have even *seen* it."

The young man gave a radiant smile. "Do not worry. My aunts have never failed."

"Your *aunts*?"

"Well, they are not really my aunts, but--"

"Perhaps you should agree on a price," the professor interrupted. "The sooner Niko gets started with this, the better." Over dinner, for which I paid, the professor assured me that the young man's methods were better not questioned.

"I can live with that. Just how long will this take? We sail for Istanbul day after tomorrow."

"A day. Maybe two." Vance-Pickett signaled the waiter for another bottle of wine and took another sweet, crisp pastry. "These are really quite delicious."

They were tasty. I couldn't help but feel guilty, what with Jones stuck back on the ship and God knows what going on there. But guilt didn't prevent me from enjoying a good night's sleep in a blissfully demon-free hotel.

The next morning I woke early. Fortified with strong coffee, I waited on the hotel veranda until young Demetrios appeared. With him were two women. One was tiny and perhaps the ugliest woman I'd ever seen. The professor's assistant introduced her as his aunt, but surely, she must have been his great-great-great aunt. She stared at me with the shrewd, glittering eyes of a feral cat contemplating a dish of mackerel. The other woman, also introduced as Demetrios' aunt, was young--a breathtaking Greek beauty with the dark skin, dark hair, and dark, dreamy eyes immortalized in great literature and cheap travel guides. Both women wore dusty black blouses, dusty black skirts, and dusty black sweaters. They carried baskets filled with metal pots, glass jars, and clay amphoras.

"May my aunts explore the ship, Captain?" Demetrios asked. "Our plan is to lure the *daemon*, trap it, and--"

"Please. However you need to do it." I arranged for the bizarre trio to be rowed out to the *Atlantis Quest* by a crewman who carried my instructions to Jones: "Allow Niko Demetrios and his associates to board the ship. They have my authorization to do anything they want. After all, things can hardly get worse."

Then I spent the day pacing the hotel lobby, occasionally looking out at the shimmering harbor to reassure myself the *Atlantis Quest* was still there. By late afternoon I'd composed in my head a letter of resignation to the shipping company. My fantasy was to send it, and then take a long trip through Europe--by train. My plans got hazier after that, but they involved several years in England, working perhaps as a shipping clerk--anything that kept me safely on shore.

Just the sun was about to set, the dinghy bearing the demon-hunting trio appeared on the darkening water, moving slowly, inexorably toward the dock. Something about the black boat on the dead calm, blood-red sea told me that they had captured their prey. I hurried over to meet them.

Demetrios climbed from the boat waving a corked amphora and beaming. "We have it!"

"Careful!" I took his arm. "For God's sake don't drop that thing."

We helped the two women from the boat. I saw, with horror, that the little old woman now had the dreamy eyes while the tall beauty surveyed us with a feral glitter. Both women wore smiles that struck me as the very opposite of contagious.

"There is one more step to be taken." Demetrios spoke in a low voice. "My aunts must seal your *daemon* into a tiny box made of silver. I will return it, thus contained, to you."

"Excellent." Then a thought struck me. Not a very nice one, I'll admit. "Wait a minute--could you have them seal it into one of those beautiful silver lockets I've seen in the local shops?"

Demetrios turned to the women and spoke in Greek. The younger one made a sour grimace and shook her head.

"I would, of course, pay an additional fee for their workmanship."

At this, the older woman nodded with great certainty, well before Demetrios could begin a translation.

"My aunts will seal the demon into a silver locket for you." The research assistant spoke slowly, almost regretfully. "But, Captain, you must promise us that you will take the locket from our island."

"That, I promise."

The "aunts" nodded solemnly. Then the trio of demon-hunters hurried across the square and disappeared down one of the narrow side streets.

A few minutes later, Vance-Pickett strolled up. "Our friend Niko was successful?"

"Apparently so. I am to take the container they give me away with us when we leave the island."

The professor's jovial expression faded. "Yes. And I heartily urge you to fling it overboard as soon as your vessel is well out to sea."

My smile tightened. "I assure you, Professor, that I have a plan for our demon."

"Captain Clayburn? Sir?" The hotel's sleepy-eyed desk clerk roused me in the middle of the night.

I pulled on shirt, pants and shoes and hustled down to the lobby to find Demetrios looking ragged, as if he'd been in a fight. But the research assistant summoned his usual bright smile and presented a small wooden box. "Please open it, Captain."

Cautiously, I removed the lid. Inside lay a heart-shaped silver locket on a black, waxed linen string. The locket was etched with odd markings. One side had a tiny hinge that looked as though it could, with some effort, be opened. I shuddered at the thought and quickly replaced the lid. "Perfect. And what do those markings on the locket--"

"Please trust me, Captain. You don't want to know."

I handed him an envelope thick with 1000-drachma notes. Payment in hand, Demetrios ran down the hotel steps and vanished into a dark alley. I wondered briefly what the two women would do with all that money on this tiny island. Buy new dusty black outfits? Then I decided I didn't want to know that, either.

I went back upstairs. But now, with the wooden box sitting atop the nightstand, my comfortable hotel room felt somehow less comfortable. I slept, uneasily, in my clothes and was up and packing at sunrise. One of the seamen rowed me out to the *Atlantis Quest*. *My God,* I thought as we neared the freighter, *even the ship looks exhausted.*

Jones, his uniform wrinkled as if slept in, greeted me and reported, with some caution, that no further incidents had occurred. "What on earth were those two strange women up to?" he asked. "There was a terrible ruckus in the cargo hold at one point. And Benjamin claims they stole several jars of strawberry jam from the galley."

"They're welcome to the jam, and anything else they may have taken. I think they really did remove our demon." I did not mention that I had brought it back with me. Jones didn't look as though he could handle that news. "Get some sleep," I ordered.

Later that afternoon the *Atlantis Quest* hauled up anchor and we steamed East on a tranquil azure sea.

Alone in my quarters that night, I took the small wooden box from my bag and set it, carefully, on my desk. I poured myself a glass of the barely adequate Scotch procured from the hotel on Taklos. Then I penned the following letter:

My dearest Isadora,

Be assured that your trunk has been consigned to the deep, as requested. Know that you have remained on my mind throughout this voyage. Enclosed is a locket I had made especially for you by artisans on one of the Greek Islands. I am certain it will cause you to recall me just as fondly as I will always recall you.

Warmest regards,

Leland

I wrapped the box and the letter in sturdy brown paper, secured it with string, and addressed it with a firm hand. The very second we docked in Istanbul, I told myself, I'd post the locket, with its oh-so-so-tempting hinge, to Isadora Beeswit in Manhattan.

A half hour later I went up on deck. I stood at the rail

for a long time, as if admiring the moonlight dancing silver on the water. And then I hurled a small, wrapped package far out into the sea.

K.G. Anderson *is a late-blooming speculative fiction author from Seattle where she writes web content by day and pens speculative fiction by night. Her stories appear in magazines and anthologies such as Galaxy's Edge and The Mammoth Book of Jack the Ripper Stories and on podcasts (Far Fetched Fables, StarShipSofa, and The Overcast). For more of her stories visit:* http://writerway.com/fiction

Eats

Elin Olausson

It's a caress, the world that Caltha lives in. It is the light that slips down from above. When you turn your head it is the movement that multiplies in the water, catches hold of weeds and algae. When you shut your eyes at night, it is the phosphorous shimmer that glows on your skin.

It's never fully dark, her home. They have allowed her to see the cold place outside, where pointy giant reeds reach for the sky. It towers above them, the otherworld. The first time she saw it she cried and hid in Alba's hair, fell asleep that way. When she woke up she was back in safety, and the otherworld was just a bad dream lurking in a corner of her mind.

Caltha, the smallest, the one who breaks. Caltha with the greenest scales.

Lutea enjoys having her hair combed.

"That's perfect, darling. Keep going."

Caltha has strong nails; they scratch across her sister's scalp like teeth. Untangle, braid, and repeat.

"I need to be especially beautiful tonight." One of those phrases Lutea keeps using, as if she only had a limited set to choose from.

"Some need more help than others." Alba, stretched out on the Whale-rock, which isn't quite as large as the name implies. Alba, with the palest eyes and hair like frost and winter.

"Speak for yourself," Lutea spits, but Caltha thinks that they are both beautiful. Big, with fins like swaying leaves, with a shock of curls covering or revealing skin. Pumila is smaller but she's a beauty, too.

"Sisters, I'm bored." Pumila grabs at a passing mackerel, but it's too fast for her twiggy fingers. When she spins around in the water it ripples around her, and Lutea's half-made braid slips from Caltha's hands and comes undone.

"We need eats," Alba says, then leans in and pinches Caltha's cheek. "Don't we, Cal?"

Caltha nods herself dizzy, and they all laugh. She loves eats. Her sisters have told her that she has, ever since she was a tiny thing, and that a girl needs eats to grow and be healthy.

"You stay here." They tuck her in, wrap her in leaves and petals. They stick dream-flowers in her hair to keep her safe.

"And no peeking," says Lutea as she always does, though they all know it's unnecessary since Caltha would never break the rules. As they leave she watches their tails, blue and white and coral. Alba once told her that tail colors can reveal people's minds, but Caltha has no idea what each color stands for. *Hunger*, she thinks. *Green stands for hunger*.

Finding eats takes time. The weeds lull her to sleep and when she awakes they are back, the sisters, chattering as they divide their finds into four equal-sized piles.

"Not too fast," Alba warns before gesturing for Caltha to dig in. "It's not going anywhere."

"Not anymore." Pumila chuckles before burying her face in a gooey, dripping piece. Caltha reaches for her own serving and grabs a chunk. It's pale-looking but meaty, and her teeth sink into the softness. She eats quickly, despite Alba's warning, and sucks the bones dry when she's done. The food goes to sleep inside her belly like a little pet and she leans back to sleep with it.

"Littlest sister." The others laugh, before sweeping their tails around her like a protective hand, hiding her away.

The changes course through her like waves, like the sea-roof changing color. One day her breasts start to grow and the next her hair darkens, as if it was just waiting for a chance to do so. Her sisters titter but she's still a child to them, and she's not allowed to help find eats. When they're away she lies half-dreaming, reeds tickling her arms and cheeks. When they return, she devours her fill.

One day, Lutea tells Caltha to swim to her. Her nails run through Caltha's hair, soft and sharp all at once, and she talks about the otherworld.

"I don't want to hear," Caltha tries, but Lutea slices through her words as if they're bubbles, air.

"The otherworld is for eats, darling. You like eats, remember?"

Caltha can't imagine all that soft and chewy coming from the nightmare-land above.

"Only a glimpse today." Lutea puts a flower behind her ear. It's red like the inside of her sisters' mouths, nothing like the dream-flowers.

"We're going up there?"

"You can't stay a child forever." Alba's white tail curls around her like a jellyfish, all silky movements. "You can't depend on others to feed you."

They swim close to her on the way up. Caltha's little heart twists and hammers like it's trying to squeeze out of her chest, out of what lies ahead. The surface is beautiful, a mirror of the sea-floor but light where it is dark, restless where it is still. She doesn't mind the surface, she just doesn't wish to go further.

"Take a look now, Cal," Pumila hisses in her ear. "But don't stick your head up too far."

Caltha looks to Alba and Lutea for guidance, but only their bodies are visible—they are facing the otherworld. Caltha pleads for her heart to stay quiet, then breaks through the surface. All at once she's attacked by noises, screeching and whining, and she retreats back down.

Alba comes after, grabbing her shoulders. "It's only the gulls," she says, stroking Caltha's hair. "It's only the wind and the crashing of the waves."

Caltha wants to cry, but she's half-grown now and not a baby. "I don't like the otherworld."

"It's where the eats come from, remember? Now come back with me, and I'll show you something nice."

It's less scary the second time. Alba points out the seagulls and says they won't harm her, because they're not big enough. She says the pointy-looking reeds are called trees and that the humans like them.

"What's a human?"

Her sisters laugh, showing teeth and tongues. She's reminded of the flower in her hair, the mouth-red petals.

"Cal, little Cal." Pumila slings an arm over her shoulder and turns her to the right. Strange beings are moving on the rocks, right next to the water.

"Humans," Lutea says, grinning. "They have no need for the sea but they crave it anyway."

Caltha can't take her eyes off the confusing sight. The creatures on the rocks are part girl, part something else — where their tails should be there are two slender, oddly shaped extremities that remind her of eels.

"What happened to them?" she asks, staring as one human moves stiffly toward the other. "Did someone cut their tails in two?"

"They don't have tails!" Pumila bursts into a fit of giggles. "They are born looking like that."

Caltha turns her eyes toward their faces, the faces of those strange new beings she never knew existed. One of them opens her mouth to say something, and the other one laughs. Her skin is dusted with freckles, sun-marked, tan.

Her teeth have no sharp edges, and the inside of her mouth is pink.

"Now go back down and wait, Caltha." Her sisters pull at her arms, turn her away from the rocks. "We will be there soon."

Caltha is disappointed—she never knew about humans until now and she wants to see if they can do anything else but laugh. Disobeying is unthinkable, though, so she swims back to the bottom of the sea. Waits, dreams, until her sisters return with fleshy piles of eats.

"You've been good." They hand her the best parts, smile as she chews the bones clean. "Soon you'll be hunting with us."

Caltha strokes the eats with her hands and likes that they are freckly, sun-marked, tan. They remind her of the humans from before and she closes her eyes and wishes that she will get to see them laugh again.

"You're going to the otherworld on your own," Lutea says one day, wrapping her tail around Caltha so that the colors mingle, coral and green. "Any day now."

"What for?"

"You don't want to?" Lutea chuckles, a sound like fingers brushing over skin. "You're a strange little thing."

"Find eats," Pumila says, swimming up to them, grinning with her red mouth. "Watch the beach until you find something, then come down to get us. We'll show you how girls hunt."

Alba joins them and grabs Caltha's hand, starts filing her nails. "You want them sharp, Cal. Sharp and strong."

Caltha doesn't know if she's ready, but she wants to be. Before she goes to sleep she gazes toward the surface, the border to the otherworld. It winks at her with a million beady eyes, and she falls asleep dreaming about humans.

#

The sisters let her know it's time some days later. They doll her up and urge her to be safe, stay out of sight. They adorn her tail with shells and flowers.

"Find us something juicy," Pumila says and giggles in her ear. "I'm starving."

Caltha pushes herself upward, enjoying the warm water caressing her face. The surface seems to call her, beckon her, and she increases her speed. Why was she ever scared of the otherworld? That fear is a distant memory now, part of the baby-days just like the ones they used to call Mother and Father.

The otherworld noises attack when she comes out of the water, just like last time, but she knows they can't hurt her and after a while her ears stop aching. The gulls soar so far above her head that she can barely see them, then dive down into the waves. One comes back up with a herring caught in its beak, and Caltha realizes why she's here. Are gulls eats? She ponders the idea for a moment but no, they look mean and they're much too small. Eats must be something that grows by the waterline, near the place where she saw the humans. She swims closer, eagerly scanning the area in front of her. It's all rocks and sand. Nothing edible.

She ducks below the surface when a human steps out on the beach. She's much closer to land than she was that other time, with the sisters. Can the human see her? Hiding among the reeds she risks another look.

It's a man. Caltha never knew there were human men — males are rare in the sea and she's only ever seen a few. He's tan like that laughing girl and his skin looks soft, like the top of the Whale-rock. His hair is black like Pumila's and Caltha would like to touch it, just to see what it feels like.

"Who's there?" He turns his head and looks right at her. She must have moved, too eager to get a better look at him. "Where did you come from?"

Caltha opens her mouth but there are no words, as if her insides have dried. The man smiles, taking a step closer.

"I'm not dangerous."

Caltha looks into his eyes and something twists in her chest, a heart bursting. She reaches her hands out but then remembers she's here to find eats for her sisters. The news about the man might make them less angry with her for failing.

She dives back into the water with a splash, speeding down. They swim toward her, hair braided, nails like claws.

"A man!" She stretches her arms wide to show them the size of him, and Lutea laughs.

"Very good, Caltha. On your first try."

"He's the prettiest thing I've ever seen." Caltha struggles to keep up with them as they move toward the surface. Blue, white, and coral. "He talked to me."

The sisters laugh and she laughs, too, because why shouldn't she? In the otherworld they swarm around her, touch her shoulders, kiss her hair.

"Now go to him, Cal, go to him. Make him come into the water."

She doesn't have to do more than smile. It seems human men like smiles a lot because he jumps to his feet and moves toward her, and she doesn't think that split tail looks so weird after all. Her skin tingles when she looks at him and she wonders if she could bring him into the sea, if she could keep him in her arms forever.

Then her sisters sidle up to her hissing about nails and mouths and *eats*, and she realizes that the drumming in her chest is hunger, and that he is soft and juicy and everything she could ever want.

Elin Olausson *is a fan of the weird and the unsettling. She is the author of the short story collection Growth and has had stories featured in The Ghastling, Luna Station Quarterly, Nightscript, and many other publications.*

Reina del Mar

J. L. Royce

Consuela Marroquín, Governor of Nuevo Colombia, drew in a slow breath. "Just because we've heard no news from outsystem doesn't mean our relay is malfunctioning."

"*Señora Gobernadora*, you *must* authorize a repair mission immediately!"

The Trade Minister's performance was for the Council's benefit. They murmured even now.

Consuela leaned across the polished burgundy table. "Our orbital fuel reserves are already low. What we *must* do is consider the cost of a launch."

The Minister withdrew. Working part-time at a forge gave Consuela a physical presence. She glanced at her Defense Minister for support.

The slight, ramrod woman with the close-cropped gray hair followed her lead like the good soldier she was.

"We don't need off-world resources—except lander fuel. The war is hundreds of parsecs away across the Arm and we've had no visitors to our system. Remote diagnostics from the relay remain nominal."

The former Marine's calm analysis had the desired effect, but Trade pressed on.

"It's bad for commerce…"

Consuela shook her head. "And the off-world market will *never* develop beyond military consumption until the Commonwealth settles the conflict."

She turned to Defense. "Please prepare a mission profile. Look at the cost and the impact on fuel reserves. We'll take the matter up again next month."

Felicia nodded, scribbling a note on her pad. It was enough to quiet the Trade Minister.

"Which leaves us with the matter of the sea…incidents."

Consuela had almost said *monsters*. What should have been just another arbitration between the mariners and owners had taken on a personal tone when the contingent of sailors arrived.

The Governor nodded. "Mr. Gonzalez Lopez represents the *Union de la Marina Mercata*." A sailor stepped forward, glancing around, a cap clutched in his hands.

The maritime representative was a wiry man, burned brown by years at sea. His companions were all sailors, men and women unused to meetings and schedules and speeches. Consuela's eyes drifted past them to a tall, familiar figure in the back of the group.

He smiled at her. She looked away.

The representative launched into a disjointed account of the (presumed) disappearance of two ships: an ore carrier, and a trading schooner, the *Gaviota*. The Council members listened patiently until Gonzalez's speech trailed off.

Consuela glanced around the Council table.

"Comments?   Suggestions?"   The   bureaucrats surrounding her were silent. But a hand went up among the guests. She swallowed.

"It appears our friend, Captain Efrain Manuel Conde, would like to address the Council. Most of you know Captain Manuel is a marine biologist and master of a ship which has sailed deeper into Pacifica than any other." She paused. "It is a…pleasant surprise to have him join us."

"*A la orden*." Efrain said, his gaze lingering on the Governor. "Council members, our ocean is vast and largely unexplored, and the loss of any ship would be a tragedy."

His voice was low and smooth, and brought back memories for Consuela quite unrelated to maritime safety.

"I've researched the marine life of Nuevo Colombia for fifteen years. Your sightings of sea life are quite plausible; but none of the indigenous forms we've encountered would attack a vessel, much less be capable of sinking it. A squall; equipment failure; navigational problems; a freak accident: these are all much more likely. And for all we know, either or both vessels will return, with stories to tell."

The captain turned to Gonzalez.

"My friends, I suggest that the Union work with vessel owners—plan voyages jointly, perhaps with convoy arrangements for at least a season."

The Union representative nodded, though still frowning. "That would be…a start. But the owners must overcome their selfish, competitive—"

"We've sailed thousands of kilometers around our world safely and will continue to do so. I'll share my navigational data to help *all* the captains plan routes." Efrain flicked a finger across his pad to toss a map to the wall screen. The assembled murmured at the methodically annotated routes. "And here are our next destinations, should any vessel wish to convoy with us."

The Trade Minister nodded. The competition to serve the planet's scattered settlements was, at times, acrimonious, but all parties respected Efrain. Consuela realized she *might* just owe him a thank-you.

"Excellent, Captain," the Minister said. "The Union representative will publicize the offer?"

Gonzalez realized she had drafted him into assisting the Council. He nodded.

"Very good." Consuela tented her hands on the table, dismissing Efrain with a nod. "Thank you, Captain."

"Next month, we review production figures—" she glanced at the Interior Minister "—so please distribute them well *before* we gather—no surprises."

Consuela frowned. "We will also have quarterly birth rate data to review."

No one expected good news. The Health Minister appeared eager to speak, but Consuela continued. "And we *will* take up the proposal for an expanded medical center at Aterrizaje."

"Other business?" She scanned the table. "Move to adjourn?"

Felicia assisted with a motion, which was seconded.

"*Padre?*"

The priest rose and lifted a hand in benediction. The Council members fell silent and bowed—*no unbelievers in politics.*

Consuela's mind was far from calm, considering the threats of crop failures, epidemics, and isolation. And looming large: *What if we simply ... fade away?*

Her worries made the unannounced arrival of an ex-lover seem trivial.

The Council members signed themselves, and rose, chatting as they left to enjoy a pleasant evening in the planet's capital.

Consuela hung back. Efrain stood with Felicia at the sweeping window overlooking Boca de Fuego's great circular bay. *Reina del Mar* lay anchored at the mouth of harbor.

"...twin electric motors, dual-mode. In a stiff wind, under full sail, we make ten knots and still harvest ample sunlight for charging the fuel cells."

Efrain gazed at his ship with a lover's fondness. As they watched, the sun sails rustled and furled for the night.

"I've never been out of sight of the coast," Felicia said.

"Then you'll need to join us on a voyage! Sail with us to the next port, take a flitter back." As he watched Consuela's approach, he lowered his voice. "Your boss needn't even know you've gone."

Consuela placed a hand on Felicia's shoulder. "The romance of the sea. Just don't eat a big meal before you experience it, *querida.*"

She turned to the captain. "Before you go, I'd like to…go over the details of your proposal."

Felicia eyed them speculatively. Shaking Efrain's hand, she promised to be in touch, and strode out with her military gait.

The two remained staring across the shimmering bay until the last Council members left.

Efrain chuckled. "*My proposal?*"

"You might have warned me."

He raised an eyebrow. "It's a free port, public meeting…"

Consuela peered sidewise at Efrain. He was heavier around the middle, yet as muscular as she remembered. "I expected you'd be sailing to Baranquilla next, but it wasn't on your chart."

"No; not this trip." His gaze remained on his vessel.

"Not going home? I thought…"

Efrain glanced at her. "I don't keep a house there anymore—we've separated. All my trips; and I plan to circumnavigate the globe on a northern route. She simply wanted someone around more, who'd try harder to start a family…"

"*Lo siento,*" Consuela murmured.

"I'd given up hope of having children." The captain shrugged. "Everyone belongs somewhere. I belong out there, on the sea. I wouldn't be much of a marine biologist if I didn't love it."

He smiled. "And you?"

"I have a place just east, on the coast—beautiful sea view, the coffee plantations stretching north at our backs…"

"So, you have someone."

"Just a roommate," Consuela said. "Well, she's more than a roommate, but that's what we tell people… Juanita's an artist, likes her solitude—almost my opposite—but we get along."

Efrain was nodding, eyebrows raised. Consuela added, "We keep our relationship to ourselves, don't hold on to each other too tightly…"

Consuela shifted her feet. "You look well…the sea air, I suppose."

"You've barely changed," he replied. "More…assertive?"

"*Boca grande, gran culo*—isn't that how you used to put it?"

He laughed. "Not in so many words. I wouldn't change a thing about you."

Consuela abandoned her irritation. "Thanks for coming, for helping. It's a good plan. Were you serious about dinner?"

Efrain faced her. "Here's my proposal: a bit of dinner, a jug of wine, and then—"

"Dinner." Consuela controlled her expression. "Quite a stroke of luck, that you just happened to be in port."

"I wanted to see you, Lela," Efrain said. "I knew the Council would be in session."

"Pretense. Why should I trust you?" But when his hand drifted around Consuela's she didn't resist.

"For old times…"

The placid bay glimmered in the waning light. A light breeze drifted in, redolent of the sea. One of the many bayfront *tabernas* had provided a lively setting for their simple dinner. The conversation had flowed with the wine, and as it did, they slipped back into their old familiarity.

"There *is* something I'd like to show you, on the *Reina*," Efrain told her as they lingered, watching the sunset. "It doesn't have to be now—I'm in port for several days. But if you like, we'll row out."

Consuela opened her pad. "Tonight is fine. Won't take long, I suppose." She jotted a brief message and swiped it closed. "Just so Juanita doesn't worry."

At the dinghy, Consuela had insisted on taking the oars. The rhythm of rowing was a relief after the Council meeting and tense week. Efrain slouched in the bow, head sagging to his shoulder and eyes half-closed, serenading his oarswoman in a strong if off-key baritone.

"*Minha canção é saudade, Do amor sonhado em vão…*"

"Is that *Portuguese*?" Consuela asked. "I don't know what's worse, your pitch or your pronunciation."

"I'm crushed," Efrain said.

"Did you have to park your boat so far out?"

"*Moored* the *ship*." He waved the jug of wine at the schooner, a shadow low on the horizon. "It's quiet out here."

"The song—where did you even hear it?" Consuela asked.

Efrain shrugged. "Someone I once knew."

She could feel his amused eyes watching her. "What?"

"Nice pectorals. You're keeping in shape. Admirable, in a bureaucrat. But if you're getting tired…"

"Not a chance," Consuela said. "My second job is hot and physical."

"Hmm. The imagination runs wild…"

Consuela scowled. "Metal working. A forge."

"So, you're making jewelry? Sounds like a pleasant hobby—"

"Parts for farm tractors, *Babosa*! The blades and struts and such—we have so many jobs unfilled. And I do horseshoes, for the farriers."

Efrain scowled. "Horses. It would have been more sensible to introduce donkeys."

"I *like* horses—very practical on the plantations."

"Like your *Papá*." Efrain said. "I never earned a *centavo* as a marine biologist. Just hauling cargo. Pull in by the anchor line—you should see a ladder."

Consuela strained to turn the small boat. "Our makers can print their own replacement parts, and commodity semis like sun-cells. Soon we won't need any parts from off-world—except quantum circuitry."

The captain grabbed the anchor chain and drew the dinghy close into the polished burgundy side of the *Reina del Mar*. He tied off the boat and pulled in the rope ladder, steadying it as Consuela climbed. On deck, she accepted the lantern and jug. Efrain joined her.

Consuela gazed back at the town as they leaned on the taffrail. Efrain stood close beside her, and she didn't draw away.

The rings of streets ascending the caldera wall of Boca de Fuego still twinkled with lit windows. On the far side of the ship, the calm sea reflected the great bowl of the cloudless night to create an illusion that they were floating in the depths of space.

"It's quiet out here," she said.

"Crew's on shore leave. We have the entire ship to ourselves…"

"You know what I'd like to see, some day?" Consuela said. "A *moonlit* sea—like Old Earth. Light everywhere on the water. Magical light, like in the stories."

"Well, we have *Via Lactea*, visible *every* night." He pointed at the jug. "And wine. I'll get some glasses."

He descended into the Captain's cabin at the stern, leaving Consuela to consider her course. She'd warned her partner she might not be home tonight.

Efrain reappeared, towels over one arm and glasses in his hand, dressed in trunks.

"What's this about?" Consuela demanded.

"A little swim—I told you I wanted to show you something." He handed her two glasses, then filled them from the jug.

"But first," he declared, "a toast: *Salud, dinero, amor.*"

"*Y tiempo para gastarlo,*" Consuela added.

They sipped, and Efrain nodded. "Where *has* the time gone?"

"Out to sea," she replied, with casual cruelty.

"Off to school," Efrain countered.

Consuela frowned. "Why shouldn't I—"

Efrain bent down to cut her off with a kiss.

"Come on," he said, "Let's take that swim. Like old times."

"I don't have a suit," Consuela objected.

"Very well— like old times!" he said. Efrain pulled down his trunks and stepped out of them.

Consuela laughed and wriggled out of her blouse, then her skirt and underwear. Efrain walked to the opposite rail and stood gazing into the darkness.

"Come here."

She strolled over to him, shivering in the cool breeze, and let down her hair, shorter now than that summer they had spent together, falling just to her shoulders. About to invite him below, Consuela fell silent when she saw the waters beyond the ship.

The ocean glowed brighter than the sky.

"What is it?" she whispered.

"What I wanted to show you."

"I've never seen the bay like this. It's beautiful; but why—"

Efrain silenced her with another kiss. "I'll show you. Let's swim."

"I have a better idea. Do you still have that dreadful hammock?"

"Yes." He took her hand. "Are you sure?"

"I didn't row all this way just to swim." She led Efrain him down the steep steps, wine bottle dangling from her free hand, into the darkness of his cabin.

Consuela slept as soundly as she had in years, cradled in the rope netting with a rough blanket folded beneath and over them. She dreamed of the summer they had shared in Baranquilla, returning after her freshman year at University. In her absence, Efrain had grown as strong and dark as a tree, working the docks as an *estibador*. They had danced around each other, day after day, until a sultry afternoon in the stifling boathouse of her father's estate.

The threat of a summer squall drove them off the beach and into the shelter. Consuela took him, unplanned and unprepared, and found everything they did as sudden and disruptive as the storm. The syncopation of fat raindrops on the boathouse roof had been impossibly loud. She could hear it still…

Consuela opened her eyes and stared into the muted blue-gray gloom of the cabin. The noise had stopped — if it wasn't just her dream. Through a port, she could see the rim of the bay twinkling with navigational lights. There was no rain.

Efrain was curled behind her, a heavy arm around her waist. Though she wanted to sleep, she wanted this more: his slow breathing in her hair, his hand warm on her belly. She wanted his body as a bulwark she could lean into without fear of falling, of betrayal. It was all an illusion, she knew, but she wanted it, anyway.

Then there was the matter of the wine they had drunk, and her bladder.

She carefully disentangled herself, found the lantern, and made her way to the tiny head. On her return she lingered, considering Efrain's life all around her, practical and beautiful.

The walls were a jumble of charts and sketches: landscapes, routes, ink drawings of the creatures of their adopted sea. She admired them one by one, the steady lines and exquisite stippling, holding the lamp close to appreciate every detail.

In the middle of the exotic alien life, Consuela found the portrait.

The pencil sketch showed a woman leaning on the ship's rail, a rugged coast behind her. Sun-bleached hair framed a pale face, at once attractive and ineffably sad, staring off across the limitless sea.

"Lela?" came Efrain's sleep query. "*Que es, amante?*"

"Nothing," she said, turning back to him. "I'm coming—"

A flash: and something landed with a splosh at her feet. It writhed, glowing, and seemed to gather itself.

Consuela squealed and scrambled back towards the hammock. Muted wet sounds came through the deck above her head.

"Something flew through the window!" she cried. It was crawling towards her, inchworm fashion, a dozen centimeters long. Then Efrain embraced her, and she tipped backward into his arms.

"Don't be afraid—they're harmless," he said. As soon as she had settled next to him, he reached over Consuela and dangled his arm over the floor.

"Don't!"

The opalescent creature moved towards his wriggling fingers, reached them, enveloped them. Efrain brought his hand up to eye level.

"Meet the genus *Psychienosi*—'messenger'. I named this species after you— *Psychienosi Consuelesis.*"

"Thank you—I think." The messenger stretched along Efrain's forearm and set up a pulsing rhythm in its pastel coloring.

"The Class *Synozoa*—cooperative sea creatures," Efrain said. "They survive without preying on higher forms; they feed on a plankton-like species. The *Psychienosi* evolved to communicate between species—with neurochemical bridging."

"Intelligence?"

"In a communal sense." Efrain brought his arm closer, but Consuela shrank back.

Another messenger appeared in the open port and made its way towards the anchor of the hammock.

"Trust me." Efrain returned his hand to her abdomen.

A warmth spread through her belly as the creature moved over her.

"They adapt rapidly to new species—including us."

The second messenger reached the hammock, then her foot, and slid along her leg.

She laughed, her fear dissolving into excitement.

Efrain was explaining neurochemical bridging as a survival adaptation, but she no longer listened. More messengers appeared, slipping over and between their bodies. Consuela felt a growing sense of *belonging*: with Efrain, with the sea beyond, with its inhabitants.

The room brightened, as more messengers joined them, drifting in from above, falling on them like a warm, heavy rain. Efrain's hands glowed, his fingers leaving patterns of light as they crossed her body. She urged him back inside of her and drifted in a kind of fugue, from frightening peaks to valleys lush and languorous.

She was Consuela, or Efrain, or the nameless *other* who traveled with them, until finally they succumbed to sleep.

Consuela opened her eyes, this time to a true, gray daybreak. The creatures had vanished, their magical light a memory—or a dream.

A dark shape moved about: Efrain.

"*Volver,*" she murmured, "*te quiero…te deseo…*" She opened her arms.

"Good morning to you, too." Efrain leaned in to kiss her.

She held his tanned face in her hands. "Was it real?"

"It's more real than you can imagine."

"How did they learn to…do that, with us? From you?"

Efrain shook his head. "It's getting light, and we haven't taken that swim."

"You and your swim! I can't get up," Consuela groaned. "My legs are like…jellyfish."

"I found something you could wear." Efrain tugged her to a sitting position on the edge of the hammock and draped a short robe around her shoulders.

"It's that, or nothing, to wear on deck. My trunks wouldn't fit you—I mean, flatter you."

Consuela slipped into the robe. "I was admiring your drawings—you should publish a collection."

"Too busy."

"I noticed a sketch…of a woman. A passenger?"

His eyes moved directly to the portrait. "A mutual friend asked me to give her passage. And yes, you're wearing her robe."

Consuela waited. "And did she have a name?"

"She went by Celeste—she was amnesic, so we never really knew. I tried to get her back to her people, on Brasilia—but…"

"What happened?"

"I failed her."

Efrain sat heavily on the trunk. "It was three seasons ago, at the peak of the war activity. She was a refugee singing in bars, lost, really; never fit in." He stopped.

"And you were lovers?"

"Yes, Lela—eventually."

His words rushed away from the memory. "Celeste was unhappy; what she called *saudade*. What I offered wasn't enough. Then she was gone."

"She made her way off-planet?"

"I thought she was coming to terms with her situation, looking forward to emigrating. We were far out at sea, I came back up from below decks, and…she was gone. Nowhere on the ship. She'd slipped over the rail. We were lovers, yes, but she was unhappy, and then she was gone. I searched—I drove the crew, I was obsessed, we scoured the ocean."

Consuela stroked his cheek. "I'm so sorry—"

Efrain took her hand. His sadness had passed as suddenly as a squall. "That's not the end of the story."

"These creatures—the messengers—are they always here, in the bay?"

With sunrise, the sky had lightened to an azure promising a lovely day. They sat with feet dangling off the deck as Efrain moistened the snorkel masks. He insisted that Consuela had to see for herself what lay beneath the surface.

"No; they followed us in from the deep ocean where their aggregates—colonies, associations—anchor. The *Bathymnemi*, their coordinators, organize these temporary aggregates, promiscuously exchanging information around the world. You saw my sketch of the whale-like creatures?"

She nodded, recalling the drawing.

"*Megalotaxidyoti*—travelers, migrating around the world, singing songs that take years to repeat: they provide transportation for all the species. And there's *Microvoythous*—microscopic helpers. The swarms are like programmable chemical plants, molecular printers."

He handed Consuela a mask and tube.

"Their culture, their literature, their knowledge—all in constant motion—maintained for millions of years! They've survived the near-destruction of their planet several times—by an asteroid, once; by warring surface dwellers, more than once."

She stared. "What—how can you know this?"

"You'll see."

Consuela recalled Efrain, painting her body with liquid light dripping from his hands, and shuddered, the future a blend of excitement and fear. She slipped out of the robe, and Efrain helped her down the side and onto the rope ladder. He dove past her, surfaced, streaming water, tossing back his hair.

"Come on—we'll want to be back on board when the crew returns."

Heart pounding, Consuela slipped beneath the surface.

The messengers gathered around the humans floating in the crystal waters. In their natural element, the creatures jetted effortlessly around the visitors, playful and familiar, touching them and each other. After their greeting, the creatures disappeared *en masse*.

She looked to Efrain, who gestured with his hand: *wait*.

From the direction of the open ocean, the water was brightening, a writhing cloud that resolved into messengers, surrounding a form, shimmering with luminescence. The being floated effortlessly towards them, propelled by the messengers flanking it, and resolved into the form of a woman, familiar and alien: Celeste.

She could have been an angel, gleaming with heaven's fire. Her pale hair floated behind her, long and unrestrained, a cloud around a beautiful face, smiling in welcome, eyes aglow. What had once been Celeste opened her arms, and Efrain propelled himself into her embrace.

Consuela felt herself drawn forward by messengers curling around her. The living fire that was Celeste extended an arm in invitation. The messengers swarmed between them, eliciting patterns in the shimmering form.

The being before her wasn't breathing. Consuela reached out to touch Celeste, but found no solid surface, for her body was alive with iridescent life—a colony of helpers.

A mix of fears overwhelmed Consuela: fear of drowning, fear of loss, fear of the unknown intimacy she faced. She struggled to remain calm as she joined Efrain in Celeste's embrace. The sea creatures welcomed them, enveloping her; and as they did, the boundary between *self* and *other* dissolved; and with it, Consuela's tension.

So much fear; unnecessary fear.

The thought wasn't Consuela's, yet it was in her mind. She whirled through a confusion of roles: sister, lover, teacher, servant, friend. She drifted closer, feeling something open through the agency of the messengers, and receive this stranger, more than human.

A flood of impressions washed through Consuela. There was the *Reina*, and the moment the woman without a home climbed over its rail to escape her demons, only to became …something else. Celeste's story unfolded as rich as a memory: the taste of the ocean, her lungs filling, the welcome oblivion…

Celeste had awakened to a new life. Helpers revived her, concentrating oxygen to her alveoli, replacing the dying organs of her body. Then they brought her to an aggregate, a place of Deep Remembrance.

The human generations on their planet were but a moment in that long remembrance, yet the ocean cared, and prepared to use what had been Celeste as its ambassador to the latest sentient species to walk the surface.

For the ocean cared…

#

Someone was shaking her. Consuela opened her eyes to the limitless sky. She tasted the sea, filling her nostrils. She coughed. She was lying naked in a puddle on the deck of the *Reina*, Efrain crouched over her.

"I thought I'd lost you! You weren't breathing — got you on deck, started heart massage. Was about to get the defib —"

"Thank you, not today," she croaked, struggling up.

"How do you feel?" He helped her into a sitting position, wrapped her in the robe, pushed damp hair out of her face.

"My throat is raw."

"Your snorkel slipped; you took in some water."

Consuela nodded. "Help me below?"

Curled in the hammock, she sipped her coffee while Efrain prepared breakfast.

"I saw so much," she said. "The more I think about it, the more I remember — or imagine? Is any of it real?"

"I have no doubt. You see why I brought you to meet her first-hand? You'd never have believed this story otherwise."

He sat and placed a tray on his knees between them. Consuela ate eagerly.

"Her memories span millions of years!" she said. "Hope and disappointment, watching the life above the waves, seeing the cycles of intelligence rising and falling, destroying themselves, or being wiped out…"

Consuela studied the wall of drawings. Another image appeared, unbidden.

"I saw a shining tower," she recalled, "rising from the ocean's floor to the sky. It was built in, in *hope,* and all manner of these creatures swarmed over it. And people! I remember humans there, too. But is it a city, a temple …"

Efrain shook his head.

"It's a radio mast, over a mid-ocean vent—geothermal powered. After we met, and they understood our technology, they tailored helpers to manufacture semiconductors, grow power circuits, microwave circuits. They built it for us—a satellite transceiver. We're using it to filter the orbital relay—"

"Those missing boats?"

"Ships," Efrain said. "Yes, the crews are assisting, voluntarily—eagerly."

"Why? Why cut off our planet?" She wanted to feel outrage but could no longer *find* it.

He took her hands in his. "They're doing it for *us*. To give us time to come to terms with everything—without interference from the Commonwealth—you can see that, can't you?"

Consuela pulled free of Efrain, shuddering.

The captain pleaded. "Nothing's changed outsystem, I can assure you. I've been monitoring interstellar traffic— I'd have told you immediately if anything was wrong! The war drags on, far away."

She shuddered. "How can I trust you—"

Efrain leaned closer. "There's more. They have our genome—the genome of Old Earth, from Celeste. They'll heal us, make us *whole* again."

Consuela sat speechless. The colony's greatest threat— declining birth rate—solved.

"You don't expect *me* to explain this to the Council?" she asked. "I'd have no more luck than you."

"No," Efrain said, "but now that you understand what is to come, you'll help them accept it."

"Accept what?" Consuela picked up her coffee, sipping it; then looked up at him, wide-eyed.

"Your crew?"

"Yes, they all bear the same gift as you, now." He smiled. "They're already sharing it with Boca de Fuego, the way we shared—with their families, their lovers, the *callejera*—"

Consuela stared. "Gift?"

"The aggregates have created a variety of helpers for us. They will become part of our biome, keeping us healthy, happy. And yes, chemically communicating. But there's more—"

The color rose in Consuela's face. "They've *colonized me*?"

As soon as it began, her indignant protest faltered. She gasped as the anger triggered an endorphin-driven wave of pleasure, sweeping over her, as intense as it was unexpected.

"The Council is our priority," Efrain said. "I'll take Felicia out on the *Reina*—you're welcome to join us—she'll be a valuable ally. And you'll have Juanita to help you with the rest, of course, after you return to her …"

Consuela felt her arousal swell unbidden at the thought of sharing this with her lover—with anyone. She imagined the beach outside her home, stepping into the gentle waves with Juanita, embracing in a new baptism, the ocean aglow…

Efrain reached out to hold her. "Can you feel it, Lela?"

"*Dios mío…*" Consuela clutched herself, shaking. "You've robbed me of my anger!"

"The *Pastor* might be more difficult. It doesn't *require* sex; it's just more enjoyable. The Church will come around—isn't this the *agape* they seek?"

Efrain's eyes gleamed with tears or an inner light. "This is just the beginning! When all is ready, we'll summon the Commonwealth—declare a planetary emergency. The interstellars will come, and receive the gift, and the *Synozoa* will move out with them, through human space."

Consuela found she could not resist—did not want to resist.

"They won't let us destroy ourselves," Efrain whispered.

"The ocean cares."

J. L. Royce has published science fiction, the macabre, and whatever else strikes him. He lives in the northern reaches of the American Midwest. His work appears in <u>Allegory</u>, Fifth Di, <u>Ghostlight</u>, <u>Love Letters to Poe</u>, Lovecraftiana, Mysterion, <u>parABnormal</u>, <u>Sci Phi</u>, Strange Aeon, <u>Utopia</u>, Wyldblood, etc. He is a member of HWA and GLAHW. Some of his anthologized stories may be found at: <u>www.jlroyce.com</u>.

Lyrics from 'Minha Canção É Saudade' by Amália Rodrigues

Creatures of Salt and Soil
Lynne Sargent

She is a sparkle on the waves that I can't look away from, even when I should be spotting other tall-masted ships. I almost shout to the sailors, to tell them that there is something on the waves before remembering, like I always do, that I have no voice they can hear. Sometimes it seems like the gulls understand, so I take my shout down to a rough whisper and tell them instead, "Look, there is a woman shining out there."

Women on the seas are rare, apart from those that are dryads like me, except none of the others are like me. They are faded, lifeless. Their spirits cling to their dead trees, as we all are bound to, but they might as well be dead too. I cannot bring myself to disconnect though, to go away as they do and become empty spirits.

Seeing her shining, iridescent speck in the water, her clear life and vigor give me comfort, and I watch her all day. It is a smooth day of sailing. My tree was made into both mast and figurehead, so I can haunt either, hovering and moving in a duality of experience where I choose within the confines of my wood. As a figurehead, my breasts are full of salt-spray and as a mast, the sails slung from me billow easily. Both spots of being give me excellent vantage to spy on her. We draw closer still and I can see that she is moving through the water, smooth and graceful, propelled by a large and powerful iridescent tail.

Though the me that is a figurehead is carved in a mermaid's image, I have never seen one before. I do not think my rendering is half so beautiful as her actuality. I wonder if the crew has ever seen a mermaid before, let alone the shipbuilder that made me. We are the same and yet different. No sculptor could give me the smooth, fatty curves that she has, both obviously strong and yet so supple. Her other proportions are wrong too — or mine are. I do not know, for she is the first true mermaid I have seen despite my months on the waves. She is so much fin and face. Her chest is flat, and her mouth takes up a full half of her visage. I am carved just like the crew, except woman-softer and more firm all at once.

I start to wonder if she would be able to hear my speech. The ache of missing the chatter of the forest that had become dull with time becomes sharp once more. More likely though, she, like the sailors, would only see a voiceless ghost.

On the third day of the mermaid's glimmering the crew spies a French ship. She is named *"The Crest,"* and her dryad is carved in the shape of the unicorn. She looks at me with dead, lifeless, eyes, just like all the others I have seen.

"I'm sorry," I mouth, as the men above begin their assault, opening the cannon hatches. One of them throws an axe. It is meant for one of the ties above her, but misses and ends up severing her horn.

"What are you sorry for?" A leisurely voice asks from the waves me, despite the din of the battle. I look down and the shining mermaid is there, through the smoke of the cannon blasts, the other dryad's horn in one hand.

I gape at her, a strange frisson running through me. It is the first time I have been spoken to in eight years. "For this," I say, gesturing at the carnage.

She shakes her head. "Surely you aren't responsible for the men aboard you."

"Without my mast holding up their sail they could not steer."

Another cannon goes off and she winces at the sound, but doesn't miss a beat of the conversation. "They use the currents to steer too, but the whole ocean cannot be said to partake in their wars."

A final cannon blast cuts off any reply I might have formulated and by the time the smoke clears she is gone, and only splinters of the unicorn and a few lost supplies remain on the waves to mark where she was.

When the carnage has settled we take their crew as prisoners for ransoming, as is customary. It is rare that anyone dies out here by anyone's hand but the seas'. Privateering is a game of economics, not one of true war. Once all of the *The Crest's* crew are safely in the brig, and whatever salvageable goods from her are aboard, my mermaid returns. She floats in amongst the wreckage of *The Crest*.

"Do they drown in you?" she whispers up to me from *The Crest's* shadow.

It catches me off guard. Both her presence, and the question. "No," I respond, finding the answer faster than I expect. "My kind makes air for them to breathe, but we can't take it from them. Besides, the crew will ransom the prisoners, not kill them. They're civilized folk."

"Civilized enough to sand a lady like you down, carve you up, and set you on the ocean?" she asks.

"They can't see me."

"Then they're blind," she says, looking at me like she can see my every ring, my every season. Looking at me like she likes what she sees.

I catch my wits and respond, "They don't see you either."

"They would if they were closer to me. Mother Ocean protects her children from prying eyes at distance and depth, but they could probably see me where I am now from the deck, if they cared to look. They get close enough to touch you and they still see nothing. That almost seems worse," she shudders.

She brings back an old ache in me, a desire to be a part of things, like I was when I had my whole forest and all its creatures living in my boughs, carrying nuts and berries and trinkets for building nests. I want her to keep seeing me. I want them to not see her, I do not want to risk this. "You'll have to be careful not to come too close then," I respond. "The men often talk of dreams of catching mermaids. They'd bring you to shore like a fish and you'd never see your home again."

"I suppose if they did that I'd be like you and your kind out here on the ocean."

I creak with discomfort. "I don't think you want to be like me. It's very lonely."

She grimaces. "Most of your kind aren't very talkative I guess. You're the first that I've met who could hold a conversation, believe me I've tried. Usually if your folk say anything at all it's just a mournful wail for leaves and birds and berries, for the caress of earthworms? Is that the word? and soil."

"Being taken from your community, and having your tree killed is…" I cannot finish the thought. It makes me want to go away, to be like the rest of the dryads on the waves. "I do miss my roots." I finish sadly, then notice the thudding of a mop and footsteps drawing closer to the prow. "Hide!" I shout.

She heeds my words and without another breath she dives beneath the waves. The man with the mop and bucket above spits over the side of the rail.

Even after this close encounter, she is back above the waves the next day, far enough out that whatever camouflage she has from the eyes of men keeps her safe. She puts on a show of diving and splashing, her tail a rainbow, her hair like a finch's plumage.

I wonder if her performance is for my benefit. I ache with longing to speak to her again.

Something stirs within me, something reciprocal, a desire to perform for her benefit — half tease, half gift. That evening I sing.

It is not something I do much anymore, it is too painful to remember the choruses of the forest — the soft ballads of growing, the rousing symphonies of storm through strong branches.

The men seem to have a similar idea and begin their own kind of song. It is bawdy raucousness, off-tune and chaotic.

"Oh, hoh, drop the anchor down
Watch the bright pretty maid as she swims round' and round'
In the day come together with swim and with play
In the night have your fun, hope there's more on the way!"

I feel my own melody fading away, giving way to theirs, until a soft gurgle, deep and succulent, mimics the last of my verses. I look down, gleeful, and she smiles up at me, moving her arms to the music's time in a languid and sensual port-de-bra. In our corner of the world, her voice buoys my song until we are the loudest here, the proximity of the waves keeping our melody apart from theirs.

We move from one song to the next, as smoothly as I cut through the night air and water, and she keeps pace with me all the while. The song of the sailors winds down, and as the sun rises and she once again floats a safe distance away I realize it is the shortest night that I have ever experienced on the waves.

We move into an easy pattern of visitation. She tells me her name is Ashera, and that she has left her home on a pilgrimage. It is something that the potential shamans of her people do in their middle years. She tells me that for the seven years she must travel the seven seas she is to speak with none of her kind.

"It's very lonely," she says, grimacing. "I thought there would be… more, but the fish just glub, and the men just shout and try to capture you, and your kind are…" she trails off. "Do they ever speak back to you?"

"No." I say softly.

I want to ask what will happen when our paths must surely diverge. I travel far, but I cannot follow her around the world. I try to muster the words, and feel myself instead becoming wooden and dead inside. My home port is Halifax, and we will turn around and return there soon enough.

Safe harbor is no place for a mermaid.

Soon, we come to realize that a ship is no place for one either. One night, in the middle of the crew's gambling, one of them drunkenly comes to piss over the edge of my prow. He aims poorly and some of it dribbles down the carved curls of my hair. It is not the worst thing that has ever fallen on me, but in doing so, he sees her.

He shouts, immediately, and nearly falls off the boat trying to get at her. Someone comes and pulls him back over the rails, giving Ashera time to dive deep and swim away. We are lucky he was drunk, otherwise the crew might have believed him, rather than laughing off his tale. But I worry about the next time, when one of them may be too sober, or have a knife or net too close at hand.

At first, I want her to stay away, and she does, reluctantly, but after a few days of silence after weeks of conversation I cannot bear it anymore, and I begin to sing our song, calling her close once more.

"How do you stand it?" she asks me one night. It is a conversation we have had many times by now.

"I don't have a choice," I respond.

"But you do choose," she says, "you stay. You don't retreat inside yourself the way the others do. You stay aware of the world."

"I made a promise, long ago to my tree. I am the caretaker, the life of this wood. They chopped the forest down, but I still stand. They killed my tree but I am still here, if not to protect, then at least to bear witness. Besides, it's not like they actually get to leave. They're still here on the waves, they just… aren't at the same time."

"Still, it might be a reprieve."

"You're my reprieve," I say.

She reaches up and places her hand on the ship's hull, just below where this part of my body meets the rest of the ship, carved maiden bleeding into seafaring vessel, merged, partial, like her. I pretend I can feel it.

We have been travelling together for weeks. Our evenings full of secret, whispered conversations. Our days, full of performance, her dancing through the waves, and me watching. She knows that when she is within my sight my gaze is always on her.

It is its own kind of language, and makes me realize how deep my loneliness has been. I do not want to lose her like I lost the forest. I do not want to become one of the voiceless dryads, lost forever inside themselves. My life has never been my own, and yet nonetheless, I have lived it. Ashera understands this too, with her pilgrimage and enforced silence. She loves the adventure of it, and yet I can tell that it is hollow for her without someone to share her new discoveries, the changing currents, the rainbow of new fish and strange creatures of the depths, the endless shorelines with wondrous sands.

On most nights we oscillate between quiet companionship and intense discussion and debate, but tonight is different, as though the wind itself has changed. She is heading up to the Artic sea next, to Nunavut, and then later over to Iceland, she has heard tales of tiny iridescent shrimp and black sands and it sounds so wonderful that I cannot take it anymore. I cannot take her joy away, cannot ask her to stay here, and yet I cannot bear to see her leave or even suggest it. And so, tonight is the night I suggest that we sink the ship.

We decide on a plan of action. It is more complicated than Ashera would like, but I insist that there must be another ship nearby so that the sailors will not drown. Every day Ashera will scout ahead. When she finds a ship that doesn't fly the Jack she will reveal herself, sing, splash, fulfill their every dream of meeting a siren. She will draw them into me, encourage a fight, telling them all sweet nothings about how she will let them have her if they can sink the ship that wronged her and imprison their crew.

In the carnage of battle she will cut me free and we will leave, together. I am nervous, but excited. My body is already dead, after all. What is it to lose a few more pieces? I worry though because Ashera is still very much flesh, and has a whole 200 years left of life, or so she tells me. She could get caught in the crossfire.

I remember the day they came to chop me down. It was early springtime, and there were a pair of chickadees mating in my branches. I remember hearing their cries and hoping that they would choose to build a nest in me too, when it was time. There are few greater joys in the world for a dryad than having your tree chosen as the home for a new family.

I had heard of the woodcutters, of course I had. Tales would pass from tree to tree. Still, I didn't think they would come for me.

I still remember how the axe felt— dull at first as it chipped away through my bark, then like a thud on my soul, the burning blinding pain as I was severed from my roots, and the world was upended as I came crashing down.

I have been broken before, first from the land, and then into two parts. Now I wait for Ashera to break me once again, so that for once I may choose my home myself, so that I may have a family who hears me once more.

The days seem impossibly long now, longer still than before I met her. She swims too far off for me to watch, and I am always, always awaiting her return at dusk.

It is the sixth day of her scouting, and when she draws closer, I see the ship she brings is called, *"La Meuse,"* and does not fly the Jack. I can tell even from this distance the blue is in the wrong place, and there is too much of it. Her portholes are already open, the cannons are primed to fire and shatter me.

A cry goes up as they close the gap between us. "At your stations! Ready your weapons!"

I can feel the hull shudder as it opens in response, feel the urgency of sails tugging against the mast part of me as they swing the boom around and pull the lines of the sail taut.

Ashera circles *La Meuse*, glancing in my direction only rarely. They draw in closer still, and begin to fire the cannons.

I feel the port side of the hull shatter first. Then another shot goes off, closer to the bow. Then, the sails swing around again and someone shouts, "Retreat!"

I am smaller than *La Meuse*. The crew must think they can outrun her, and they may be right, even with pieces in the water.

"No!" Ashera shouts, and moves towards me swiftly, amidst the smoke and shrapnel. As we rotate I feel the cannons blow, the kickback reverberating in a syncopated sequence.

Over the din, I hear Ashera shout again, but my senses are ringing and I can't hear what she says. I look down and see her below me, once again floating in splinters of wood.

A man runs over to the rails with sword and looks down, seeing her, he goes to throw the sword and I shriek. It is like the sound of sizzling lightning. I sustain the note; it is all I have. A shudder runs through his body and he stares about. I can tell the sense of his mind working through, "*A ghost? In the day? In battle?*" The distraction is enough, and another blast rings out, and suddenly I am cracking apart, figurehead separating from ship.

The pain, if it can even be called that, is blinding. Where before the cuts were linear, now I am splintering. I am hewn from myself and yet I am still myself, my mast has been left behind but I lash my spirit to the figurehead, which falls into the waves.

Ashera darts quickly out of my trajectory, the din of battle all around.

"Over there!" I shout, through the pain, directing her to a nearby net floating in the water. It is shredded in places by cannon fire, but still enough.

The men are caught up in their battle, but as Ashera wraps me, preparing me for towing a few begin to notice and shout their outrage. I begin to panic. I cannot lose her, not like this, not now. I force my ghostly form to rise out of the figurehead, reaching back to the mast on the ship. I strain, feeling each piece of me that is missing. I remember all that was left behind in the forest, roots and branches, all the things I've lost, the wounds become dull with time. I concentrate my will, then split it in two, wrenching and wailing until finally, with a great snap, the mast that once was a part of me, and perhaps still is and always will be comes crashing down on the deck, sending the men scrambling.

I snap back to the figurehead, as much of me as is left anyways, and Ashera begins to tow me from the wreckage, her face ashen with fear.

I cannot speak, I do not know if I cannot even *be*, anymore, at least not in this moment. She accepts the silence.

The days pass, and slowly I come back to myself. We stay to the deeps, away from shipping lanes.

I still cannot speak, cannot share or connect or do any of the things that made me love her in the first place, until one night we are drifting. She has laid her head upon my belly for sleep and I feel a song rising there, as though it emanates from her. The timbre of my voice has changed, become something raspy, deeper, but still beautiful.

Her eyes flutter open, and she smiles, softly crooning with me. In the morning, when it is time to continue on her pilgrimage, now ours, now shared, she asks me, "Where would you like to go?"

I point in a direction, and she follows my hand.

I am as rooted as I ever was, as bound. I am fragmented, but not lesser. I am no longer constrained by my roots, or the shipbuilders, or the sailors. I get to choose.

And so I do.

I choose the ocean.

I choose freedom.

I choose her.

Lynne Sargent is a writer, aerialist, and holds a Ph.D in Applied Philosophy. They are the poetry editor at Utopia Science Fiction magazine. Their work has been nominated for Rhysling, Elgin, and

Lynne Sargent

Aurora Awards, and has appeared in venues such as *Augur Magazine*, *Strange Horizons*, and *Daily Science Fiction*. Their first collection, *A Refuge of Tales* is out now from Renaissance Press. To find out more, reach out to them on Twitter @SamLynneS or for a complete bibliography visit them at scribbledshadows.wordpress.com.

The Tide Queen
Chloe Smith

If you dig down far enough into the sand of the beach, you'll hit bone.

Not immediately; enough time has passed. You can't simply worm your fingers and toes into the warmth of the dry, sliding surface—casual as you sit, looking down at the waves—and feel the dead beneath you. You couldn't even find them if you scoop with both hands, down to the place where the sand is still damp, where it grates under your nails as you scrape at it.

No, the bones are buried deep. A searcher would need a hole big enough to stand in, deep enough that water seeps up into it. Then, sure enough, your spade or trowel would hit a piece of bone. It might be a fragment, worn shapeless by the grind of the elements against each other. Or it might be something whole—a rib or slender forearm, or even the curved dome of a skull.

One of those skulls is my father's.

I used to wonder which one was his, back when I craved belonging so badly that I searched for any details that might anchor me in place. I imagined my lost father with the same face as the king my uncle, only warmer, nearer, and always there. If I knew where my father's relic lay, I could, I thought, feel closer to that vision.

His bones were unmarked amid all the rest, though, even when they weren't buried. The remains of fallen bridegrooms spread out from the walls of my cell, thrown back to shore by the satiated sea, scoured bare by salt wind and brushed free of shifting sand by the pilgrims who came to kneel below my slitted windows. If you had visited the beach back then, you could have joined those supplicants in their genuflections.

I remember the endless sound of their murmuring, gratitudes and prayers for protection. It blended with the sound of the waves, a counterpoint susurrus. I knew they touched their foreheads to the stone base of my tower, left offerings of braided seaweed and carved, iridescent shell scraps in honor of the strange daughter of the sea. When I was little, I liked to wave to them. I asked my uncle, during one of his daily visits, why they turned their faces away and never waved back. He told me that it was out of respect.

It was only much later that I learned to recognize it as fear—or learned to see any aspect of the world as different from what he told me.

My earliest memories are of excitement at the sound of his key in the lock. He would let himself in while his guards waited without, endure my scale-dotted, clammy arms around his knees, and then his waist as I grew taller. I would ask him to sit with me in the damp dimness and tell me again the story of myself.

He told me that I was the Tide Queen's daughter, destined to protect this beach and this land from the encroaching ravages of the sea. He told me how his brother gave his life in a great sacrifice, going down with many ships full of men, a legion drowned so that the Tide Queen would acknowledge such a rich dowry, allow him to get her with child. My uncle told me the story of my birth, as well—how I hatched from an egg among a clutch of sea turtles, tapped my way out with tiny fists, and then squirmed and cried piteously as my nestmates slid and scuttled down to the waterline. He told me how he lifted me up, swaddled me in sealskin blankets, and how the waves retreated in haste when he turned my infant face towards them.

"That was when I knew," he said, hand heavy on my sea-kelp hair. "You would be our salvation, for the Tide

Queen recognizes her own blood, and will not trespass against it."

Seated on the stone flags by his feet, I looked up at his frown. It told me that his thoughts had moved away from me, and I shivered and probed for reassurance. "But I am yours, too, am I not? I belong to the land?"

The heaviness waned as a smile folded the corners of his eyes. "Yes, my dear. You are my bulwark against the rising tide." I wrapped my webbed hands around my knobby knees and leaned against his leg, comforted—at least until his visit ended.

You may wonder how a child, even a half-human child like me, could grow up within the circular walls of a devotional cell, without ending every day scratching my claw-nails bloody against the stone blocks that hemmed me in. How could you not ask these questions?

I do not know if this trammeled life stunted me—I have no counter example, no sisters or brothers with which to compare myself—and I do remember moments when the hours stretched before and behind me like the blackest depths of the ocean, when my uncle's next visit floated ahead of me like the only faint light for me to focus on. Two things, though, kept me, if not sane, as least as well-balanced as any creature of my dual nature and inheritance.

The first was my uncle's own doing, uncharacteristic of him as it seems, looking back. He taught me to read. Our storytimes were replaced with lessons. He sat in his chair (it was always *his*, for I never presumed to sit in it, even when alone), and I sat on the floor before him and puzzled over the shapes of words on thick pieces of foam-white parchment, gradually learning how to trawl their groupings for meaning. I think he wanted me to wear a mask of civilization, even as I grew up, a grey-skinned, fish-eyed child, imprisoned beside the sea. He hoped I would learn to mimic the princesses in the stories, the patient wives and gentle mothers, and I read those tales, but I did not stop there. I begged for more books, histories and philosophies, texts that told the wars and economies of the kingdoms of the land and traced the mysteries of the charted and uncharted seas. He frowned at these requests as I grew older, threatened to leave me alone for days at a time in punishment for my unbecoming interests. I learned to court his approval, to mask the shape of my limbs in dresses of his choosing, to play the part he imagined for me.

The other way I evaded the madness of confinement — that I discovered even younger. When my child's spirit would have broken, when loneliness became a squall that wracked my body and left me gasping on the floor, the sea came to sustain me.

The waters rushed in, surged up within my soul, and my awareness of my body faded. I opened my eyes on the sunken world of shadows and fractured light.

That first time, I spasmed with fear more than wonder, even as my movements met no resistance, unleashing cascading currents with the power of my limbs. I thought my mother must have pulled me here, and I was terrified to face her, terrified that I had was somehow betrayed my uncle, betrayed my responsibility to protect the beach from her conquest. With a mental wrench I pulled myself back into my body, where seawater poured from my mouth and nose like a resurrected sailor. I huddled against the wall of my cell, within the limitations of the world I saw through my eyes and heard with my ears, and trembled with guilt.

But no consequences followed — no appearance from the Tide Queen and no hint from my uncle, on his next visit, that he'd realized what I'd done. My curiosity grew as the memory of terror faded. I began to hear again the rush and hiss of moving water within my soul as well as beyond my walls. Tempted, I closed my eyes and let the sea take me again.

Soon, I began slipping through the channels of the sea whenever the dripping stone around me grew too stifling. I explored the glass-ceilinged palaces of the ocean, moved among the teeming, silver clouds of fish and faced great, shadowy behemoths of the deep. I was always alone, except for the creatures of the water, and so I told myself it was no betrayal; that, in fact, I was fulfilling the duty I was born to, patrolling against the Tide Queen's rising influence. I didn't know, then, what freedom felt like, and so I didn't understand the buoyant joy these sojourns brought me.

The books of the land, the channels of the sea, and always, first and last, my uncle's visits and the picture of my life that he reflected back at me in the mirror of his stories—these were the pillars on which my world rested. The years passed, and while I witnessed, read, heard of change and transformation, my own existence seemed becalmed, unchanging. The pilgrims knelt beyond my walls and then went on their way; the seasons turned and turned again. Sometimes storms ravaged the beach and waves struck at the foundation of my cell, but my uncle assured me that none were as monstrous as those that threatened to rise and swamp the land before I was born.

One day, though, my uncle paused after he turned from locking my door behind him. He didn't go immediately to sit in his chair. I had already taken my accustomed place by its foot, and I had pulled a book onto my lap, careful to dry my fingers before I began turning the pages. I had some detail I wanted to ask him about. I still saw him as the first and greatest authority.

He spoke before I could frame my question, though. "Seastar," (that was the name he called me most often) "Stand, so I can look at you."

Troubled, I laid the book aside and did as he asked. I saw him wince as he looked me up and down. "It is too bad you are not more of a woman."

"I wish I did not disappoint you," I answered. That was a true regret, although I did not understand his feelings. I did not wish to have the softly rounded forms of women I had seen in pictures, or experience the inner tides of blood that I knew from my reading were an inevitable part of human womb carriers. To my mind, these qualities were like the clouds of eggs that fat-bellied fish left on the floor of the ocean or among the fronds of the sea gardens. They were all intriguing features of the world—but they had little to do with me. I had seen no parallel anywhere to the contours of my body. I was a unique hybrid of land and sea. I knew, even though my uncle had never suggested the word to me, I was monstrous in my singularity.

He sighed and crossed the space between us, looked up into my face (I used to forget, when I always knelt at his feet, that I had grown taller than him). "You know that I grow old," he said.

My breath caught, and I resisted the desire to embraced him. I'd learned to recognize his winces at my fishy touch. "You are still hale and strong!" I protested.

"But I will die," he continued.

"No!" I could not imagine my world without the shape he gave it.

"Yes. All things die. Except your mother. The Tide Queen lives on, and her hunger for the land is constant and eternal."

I felt the old shame of association and tried to fend it off. "But you have me. The beach and the land and all its people have me to protect them." I wanted him to agree, to assure me again that I was his bulwark.

He hesitated. "Ye-e-s. But you have human blood and are likely mortal as well. Someday, this world will lose you, too—not for many years, I hope—but still, we must think of the future. How can we ensure that this guardianship will continue past our lifetimes?"

My heart lifted at that "we." As much I longed for him to be a larger part of my life, I desired also to be a part of his. Had he come to include me in his kingly strategizing, that we might study together to craft a plan for future defense? Could I truly act as his daughter, even if bound within the walls of my cell? I had told myself so often that I was satisfied with the service gave, the duties I maintained merely by existing, but the idea of something more filled me with sudden hope.

"I don't know, Uncle," I began, "But—"

He laughed. "My Seastar, how could you? I wouldn't expect you to contemplate such things." I had to fight to hide the way my hope crumbled, so I almost missed his next words: "But don't worry! I have a plan."

"Will you send more men to the Tide Queen?" I asked. My voice was small, but steady, at least.

"No! That was too great a sacrifice." I must have failed, then, to control my expression, because he reached out and lightly touched the back of my hand. "Not to create you, my dear, that was worth it—but I cannot keep doing that. And I don't have to. You are the start of a new line of guardians."

It took me a moment to understand what he was saying, to connect it with his earlier regret about my lack of womanliness. "A new line?" I hoped I was mistaken.

"Yes…" He frowned, wiping the hand he'd touched me with against the leg of his trousers. "I will have to offer a third of my kingdom to any man that is willing"

I looked down at the webbed hands I clasped before me and thought of the pilgrims with their averted eyes. I imagined the touch of another man, a stranger, who might grasp me with strange hunger or trembling horror. Either possibility made my guts churn. "I do not think I am a fit match for any human man."

He mistook my confusion of shame and repulsion for a more reasoned criticism. "Oh well, if that doesn't work, my secondary plan is to put you into the sea." I looked up to see him gazing thoughtfully into space. "Perhaps a creature out of the depths can get you with child. I don't know which sire will be better to further the line I need to cultivate."

I recognized his words from terms I had read relating to the keeping of animals, and my shame curdled into rage. "I am not a fish you have caught in a weir!" I glared at him in anger I had never felt before. I bared my pointed teeth and pushed him away.

He stumbled back, and I saw his face change for a moment. He was afraid of me! I was suddenly, again, the child who had looked up for his approval, and I recoiled from myself. I sank to my knees. "I'm sorry, uncle! I didn't mean to—" I reached out one hand, saw its elongated, claw-tipped ugliness, and drew it back.

He stiffened as I crumpled. "I see I have misled you. I wouldn't have said I had encouraged you to question your place in the world, to underestimate the weight of your responsibilities—yet this is how you act? I should never have imagined you could understand."

He paused, then added. "You are my bulwark, but also my creature. I will decide what fate is best for you."

He turned while I was still too stricken to respond. I heard the door lock behind him.

I waited days for him to return, days while successive tides of hurt, regret, and anger—first at him and then at myself—washed through me. I tore the pages from my books and let them fall into the puddling water around my feet, watched the ink run and the clean paper turn to mush. I screamed and watched the pilgrims gather up their robes and flee, then screamed and screamed again, defying the veneration of any new supplicants who might approach, wanting only to make them feel the same fear and hurt as I did. Soon the only human figures I saw were silhouettes that appeared and then vanished behind the far crests of the dunes.

I thought again and again of the terror I had seen on his face, and it shifted some balance of self-awareness deep inside me. My monstrous form, the guards who would not follow him into my presence, and he—the man who'd held me as an infant, who had always loomed so large before me, even now that I stood taller than him—now cringed away, even as he sought to use me further. Those new understandings, that I was fearsome, that I was a thing to him, that I had failed him, they were a storm within me, a maelstrom so violent that I could not escape it even when I fled into the channels of the sea.

It was that violence of emotion, I think, that finally brought the Tide Queen to me.

I awoke from fitful sleep, unsure what had disturbed me, until I looked out the window slit that faced most directly onto the beach. The moon was full, and its light gilded the waves that it had pulled up, up onto the shore. The breakers crashed, and crashed again, and beyond them, where the ocean loses all relation with the land, my mother rose up out of the water.

She emerged halfway to the horizon, but even at that distance I could see her shape, tall and larger than any man, with osprey-eyed clarity. Her limbs were long as my own, and even more alien, sometimes shifting in curves and ripples of ill-defined motion, sometimes sharp and violent as the dive of a cormorant through water. Her hair was long as well, and tangled with the riches of the deep, coral and pearl, but also strands of strange plants and slippery creatures neither plant nor animal. Her eyes were hollow, the enormous cavities of a skull's, but anglerfish glows flickered in their depths.

I knew her gaze found mine, although I could not recognize it, and I fought the urge to shrink back. Instead, I held up my hand against her, invisible through I might be behind my cell's wall. "Begone!" I screamed, raw-throated, "This land is mine by birthright. You shall not have it!"

I didn't know how she could hear my words across the surf and the distance between us, but somehow she did, and her tongueless mouth opened in silent laughter.

A birthright of violence and destruction! She spoke without sound, and I heard it in the vibrating bones of my skull. *I hope you have joy of that, child. It is a heritage that separates you from me, that keeps me from taking what I will. Why else do you think I threw you up upon the land?*

"What?" I reeled beneath the wound of another realization: I had been discarded, not won.

The sacrifice of bodies thrown into the deep was sickening, even for me. An army of men drowned, and for what? That I might take one as my consort? I always take a few drowned sailors for myself, and I've had other daughters, ones I wanted, ones that I kept. Your begetting poisoned any desire I had for you.

This idea was so shattering to my vision of myself that I felt as if the air was drowning me now. "But, the heroic dead; the prince my father—" I managed.

She laughed again. *Oh, heroism! Those men whose boats were scuttled and those who were thrown from the bridge of the royal flagship, in hopes that one might bring a bastard home for the king? Yes, one of them was even his brother. His screams and pleas for mercy sounded much like the rest. It might even be his seed that reached the egg you sprang from. By then, though, the bodies and their ships' detritus sinking to the ocean floor had become too much. I wanted only to push them out onto the land again. Let humans pollute their own realm, not mine.*

And when they've done themselves to death, and you are gone, then I'll rise and take the land back. In time. Her haggard jaw gaped in a grin.

The anger that surged against my uncle was nothing to the rage that filled me now. It was a tidal wave, a wall of violence cresting. I put my hands on the narrow edges of my window and tore it wider. The rock crumbled under my grip as if years of water ate it away. I reached through the space I'd created, as if I could grasp at her across the distance. "Never! You chose to throw me away? More fool you! Maybe I'll come into the sea and take your crown from you."

A force like the deep currents of the ocean lifted my limbs. The waves arced up and roared down more violently. Their crashes echoed the sound of my words as they sent plumes of spray up into the air—but I couldn't tell if it was my power or hers that made them move so.

She laughed one more time, silently, and then sank beneath the surface of the water, giving me no hint that my threat held any weight for her. I staggered back, too, turned away from my newly widened window and threw myself into the chair I had always saved for my uncle. I cried then, salty, human tears from my fish eyes, as the truth of what I was, of what my uncle has done, settled into clarity.

I cried for my unknown father and the other dead men; I cried for my uncle's love, which might be real to him, but had died for me as I came to understand that I was a thing he owned. I cried for myself, that I was the monstrous daughter of a monster mother. I wished to die immediately, so that I could hasten the day the land would be swept away forever. I imagined plunging into the sea, to wrestle my mother for her crown, that I might take my revenge as the greatest monster of them all.

I was alone in my monstrousness, and always would be.

It is impossible for my tears to run dry, but I cried myself to sleep at last, and woke in the early light of a new day. I shifted, stiff from hours curled in the chair. The ocean and its winds were quiet for once.

In the near silence, I heard a voice, singing. I tumbled out of the chair and pulled myself up to look out the window—and I saw you.

You walked the flat, gleaming edge of the sand, where the edges of the wave could just tangle with your footprints. There was no reason for you to be there—no errand, or pilgrimage, or work to be done. Your arms swung as you walked, and your head was held high. Your skin was soft and human-round, your face open and happy. You sang for yourself and the joy of being alive and in the world.

I stood still in the shadows of my cell. I did not want you to see me, to run away in fear. It wasn't long before you passed beyond my line of sight, although your song lingered after you in the air.

I tried to remember the words and the tune after you were gone, to recreate them with my own voice. I imagined trying to keep that memory, to sing those words alone under the sky, once the sea had swamped the beach and washed away all trace of human lives. I knew I wouldn't be able to.

I weighed your joy, your song, against the knowledge my mother had given me, the horrors of so many dead, the bones that were even now beginning to disappear beneath the sands of the beach, now that the pilgrims had fled. Did the land deserve to survive forever? Was it worth the price of my body, whored out to man or sea creature?

I was still wondering, when my uncle finally returned.

I heard his key turn in the lock, even over the noise of the surf through my ruined window. I stared out at the grey line of the horizon, unwilling to see his reaction to what I had done.

"Seastar," he said at last. "I have never been more proud than on the day you were born."

The old story slid into my heart with a harpoon's vicious barb. I turned, looking for the uncle I remembered, the warm eyes and indulgent smile.

He might have still looked at me that way, but I was distracted by the handful of guards he'd brought. They flanked him, backs stiff with tension, and their hands jittered over the hilts of their weapons. It took me a moment to find my uncle's face in their midst. By the time my eyes caught his, he must have seen that he'd lost me, because his expression tightened as well.

"Why, Uncle?" I asked. Something of my mother's deep-sea power surged beneath my words. Perhaps it was that which drew the truth out of him.

"You are my legacy, my greatest achievement, my protec—"

I moved before he could finish. I knocked the useless guards aside, left them broken and dazed. I closed on my uncle, and did what I had to do.

For my survival.

I am his child, after all. He should have known I would.

In the quiet after the terrified guards staggered away, I leaned over my uncle's body. I told him, "I am not your anything."

His mouth panted open, wide as a fish. I could hear the blood rising in his lungs. I wanted to look away, to cover my ears and hide from the evidence of his suffering, just as he hid the memory of my father and the rest—the lives he sacrificed to bring me into the world. I didn't let myself flinch. I listened to the gurgle and the chop of waves.

He tried to speak, reached for me. I didn't reach back. I watched, so that I could remember what it felt like to have done this. Blood bubbled at his mouth at the last. One final, choking rasp, and then stillness. I sucked my own breath in, silently, and then I reached down and touched him, once he could no longer touch me.

Outside, as the guards fled, I crossed on the sand that I hadn't touched since I was an infant. I stood at the wave line and shouted defiance at the sea, "You cannot have the land while I stand on it!"

If my mother heard me, she gave no sign.

I hope you, or others like you, will visit my beach again. I do not know how long I will live, or when the Tide Queen may raise the seas—but for now I remain. The land and its people, for good or ill, survive.

If you return, maybe you will walk once more along the beach, singing for the joy of song. Maybe you will stop and sit, look out to sea, dig your fingers into the sand that has covered the remains of many bones, the skulls of dead men.

One of those skulls is my uncle's.

Chloe Smith teaches English and history to 14-year-olds, which is never boring. Besides teaching, she works as a proofreader for Fantasy magazine, and writes science fiction and fantasy stories whenever she can make the time. She was born and raised in the San Francisco Bay Area, and she lived in Texas and Washington states, New York City, and rural France before coming back to California. Her short fiction has appeared in Metaphorosis, Three-Lobed Burning Eye, Interzone Digital, and elsewhere. Her debut novella, Virgin Land, is out from Luna Press Publishing in February 2023.

Depth Becomes Her
Michelle Tang

Something plunged into the eternal twilight of my world, disturbing the murky depths, stirring water against my skin with vibrations unfamiliar and strange. Novelty was a rare treasure, so I roused from my half-slumber to investigate.

The sinking visitor thrashed, white-clad, trailing bubbles like an effervescent veil. I stopped my reluctant bride's descent, marveled at its unscaled flesh. I bioluminesced brighter to examine its fine features. My gaze traveled down the high forehead, the straight nose, the lips clamped closed. Hair sprouted from its cheeks and chin, short and stiff like sea urchin—not a bride after all, but a groom.

His dark eyes bulged, their color leeched away by the depths. I believed him agog at the sight of me—perhaps his world told tales of my kind the way we did of theirs. Then I noticed his desperate movements, how his heart spasmed against his chest like a fish out of water. The stream of bubbles trailing from his body had ceased.

Curiosity clutched me in its spell, so I wove one of my own. The man's mouth opened to expel the last of his air. He inhaled water. I laughed, silent as the sea bed, at his awestruck face. I untangled the rope wrapped around his legs; it coiled onto the ground like an eel.

The man moved his lips, but I only heard burbling water. I used sound waves and color changes, but he answered none of my questions. His pale hand gestured gratefully from his chest to mine. He looked around at my home, using the light of my glowing body to see. He lost interest quickly: there was precious little here, and anything of value quickly devoured.

His gaze turned to me. I tried to see myself through his human eyes: a glowing creature with wild sea-kelp hair and large, dark eyes. My lips were like his, though my nose was nearly flat. Maybe, to him, my amorphous body resembled a dress, billowing in the current. Maybe I looked human. He looked neither displeased nor afraid, baring dull white teeth. Though I was unversed in the ways of such creatures, I detected a glint of… interest in his stare.

The man used a finger—unwebbed, how strange— to point upwards. I imagined ignoring his request, keeping him here and memorizing his strange form until there was nothing left behind but bones and tattered white cloth. I thought of bringing him to the others, parading him like the strange exhibit he was, a myth made flesh. Ideas sprang to mind, anything but what he asked. Like many who lived in the deep, I had never ascended to the surface.

In the end, the beseeching look on his face and my own boredom convinced me. I grasped his arms and began to swim upwards, to shallower waters where the moon's cold silver light trickled through. The muscles in the man's body were firm, covering inflexible bones, and I wondered that I was touching this creature that water-kind only spoke of in whispers.

When I was small enough to cling to my Mare, she told me and my siblings tales of humans, frightening two-legged monsters that would catch us if we strayed too far. Fish that braved the surface described men, deadly and grim-eyed and cruel. And yet, there was talk of their beauty, their long bodies in a myriad of hues shining beneath the sun. They created wonders: things that floated, or sank, or expl

oded. It was said they could lift their voice in song.

In the silver-tinged water, he looked at me differently. His fine dark brows furrowed and his smiling lips thinned. The lower pressure had changed my shape: it happened to most deep-sea creatures who swam too high. The currents were stronger here, and I felt stretched in all directions. I shuddered a distress call, lights beneath my skin flickering different colors. I needed to leave, let the man float upwards until my magic left him, and leave his fate up to his gods.

Hearts pounding, I released him. He grabbed hold of me and kicked upwards, dragging me like a sodden blanket. I shook my head and tried to tell him I could not bear such lightness around me, but he did not heed. The flash of interest I thought I'd seen in his eyes was gone, replaced with clenched-jaw determination.

My colors flared again, brilliant and bright in the shallows. Other creatures shied away when they saw what had hold of me. I struggled to control my movements, fought to remain in my skin. I took small breaths, afraid a larger inhalation might prove too much for my over-stretched organs. I longed for the heavy compression of my seabed, comforting like the carcass of a whale, or my Mare's embrace.

The man's gaze was cast upwards towards the sky, his fists gripped painfully in my body. I threw magic at him, starting with small stinging spells that he ignored, and then, as I grew more desperate, stronger enchantments that made him scowl. He yanked his hands apart, tearing my already burning flesh, and I was afraid to try again. I could not overpower him with magic when my body writhed in agony.

I could revoke my first spell, allow the water in his lungs to drown him, and hope I could escape while he panicked. I feared he would rip me apart in his death throes.

I feared I was already too damaged to return to the safety of my home.

I feared.

Is this better than boredom? I chastised myself.

Amidst the pain of my body expanding, an idea grew. Like sea creatures, human bodies were mostly water, that element within my control. I stopped our ascent, my body billowing out to drag against his kicks, and took firm grasp of him once more.

His eyes in this light water were green, but they were colder and crueler than the ancient sharks that occasionally swam past me.

I poured myself inside him, entering with the water he breathed, and forcing my ever-expanding body inside his solid cage of organ and bone.

The man fought, of course, but he could not expel me. The pain inside my body stopped, sheltered inside a human frame. I swam upwards until I broke surface. My magic cleared lungs and stomach of brine.

I took my first breath of air.

It was like being born. His brain imparted to me many secrets, more than a century of rumoring fish. My soaked clothing chafed against my water-wrinkled skin, unfamiliar and strange. I walked towards the approaching dawn, new green eyes devouring the sights, hearts pounding in anticipation. There were treasures to be discovered.

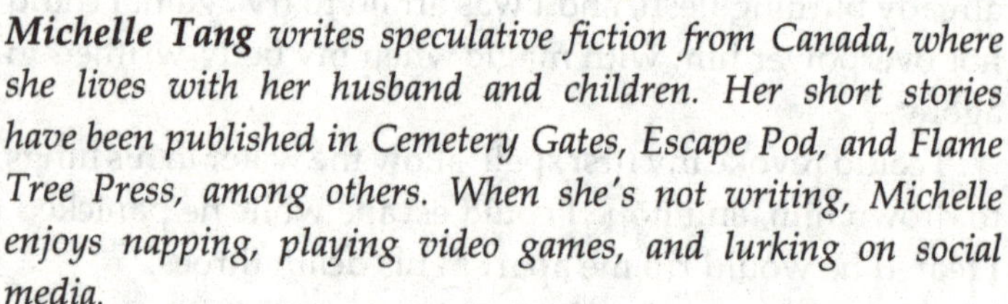

Michelle Tang writes speculative fiction from Canada, where she lives with her husband and children. Her short stories have been published in Cemetery Gates, Escape Pod, and Flame Tree Press, among others. When she's not writing, Michelle enjoys napping, playing video games, and lurking on social media.

You can follow us:

on **Twitter** (@WyldbloodPress)
on **Facebook** (www.facebook.com/WyldboodPress)
on our **website** (www.wyldblood.com)
by **email** (contact@wyldblood.com)
or by subscribing to our **newsletter**
(http://eepurl.com/haa4Zn).

WYLDBLOOD

www.ingramcontent.com/pod-product-compliance
Lightning Source LLC
Chambersburg PA
CBHW010544170726
48285CB00008B/2743